THE SISTERS

JOHN NICHOLL

ALSO BY JOHN NICHOLL

1

Detective Inspector Laura Kesey spotted the victim almost as soon as she entered West Wales Hospital's acute admissions ward. The skinny, nineteen-year-old girl was lying propped up on three plump pillows, her short, bright red hair and multiple blue tattoos contrasting dramatically against the starched white cotton covers. Kesey made a slight involuntary grimace on witnessing the young woman's battered appearance. Her two black eyes, a torn lip, the misaligned nose, and a missing front tooth transformed her otherwise pretty face into something akin to a Halloween mask. Physical injuries that were testament to the severe beating she'd received only hours before.

The detective struggled to suppress her anger as she approached the bed, her sense of injustice burning bright as she met the girl's haunted gaze. Kesey settled herself, swallowing hard, adopting a professional persona, keen to convey both approachability and calm efficiency, a combination of which she hoped would help put the young woman at her ease. Or, at least, as far as was possible in the circumstances.

Kesey had met victims like this before. Unfortunate females dominated and abused by violent, manipulative males. She'd met more than she cared to recall. And the last thing Kesey wanted was to let the young woman down. Every case mattered to the detective, and incidents such as this more than most.

The young victim removed her in-ear headphones, grimacing with each movement of her battered body, as the detective stood at the end of her hospital bed, focused on her and only her, resisting the almost overwhelming impulse to look away. Kesey shifted her weight from one foot to the other, forcing a thin smile before opening her mouth. When she spoke, it was in nasal Brummie tones that some Welsh locals found challenging to decipher.

'Hello, Sally, my name's DI Kesey, Laura Kesey. Please call me Laura. I'm here to help you.'

The young woman averted her eyes to the wall, spitting her words, spewing them from her mouth. 'Yeah, like that's going to make all the fucking difference. Why don't you piss off and leave me alone? You can't help me. Nobody can.'

Kesey held her ground. It wasn't exactly the welcome she'd hoped for. But it wasn't entirely unexpected. And she'd heard a lot worse. 'I wouldn't be here if that were true.'

Sally was visibly sweating now, tiny beads of moisture exuding through the pores of her discoloured skin as she tugged on her ginger hair. 'Oh, give me a break. Have I got stupid stamped on my forehead or something? Who the fuck do you think you are, Superwoman? I know your limitations. I've been down this road before.'

Kesey pulled up a chair, sitting to the left side of the bed, next to a large picture window with a view of the busy car park below. The detective maintained as calm a tone as possible, speaking slowly, clearly enunciating each word, monotone, bordering on the melancholy. 'How are you feeling? It looks like he really did a job on you this time.'

The young woman emitted a long, deep audible breath,

more a groan than a murmur. 'Yeah, and he'll do it again if he finds out I've been talking to the likes of you. Why don't you fuck off and ruin someone else's day? If you think you're helping, you're kidding yourself. You're just making things worse. Your sort always do.'

Kesey paused before replying, taking her time, choosing her words with care. 'Pearson's in custody, Sally. He's locked up in a cell. And with your help, we can get him convicted and imprisoned. Don't you think he deserves that after all he did to you? I know it isn't going to be easy, but it matters. We can't let him get away with it. You can be free of him. I'll be with you every step of the way.'

Sally closed her eyes tight, screwing up her face, shutting out the world. When they flickered open moments later, Kesey thought the girl may start weeping. There was an unmistakable sadness about her. An absence of hope she couldn't hide.

She looked past Kesey as she spoke. 'I've been here before, on the exact same ward, just over a year ago, at Christmas.' Sally pointed a trembling finger decorated with peeling black nail polish. 'I was stuck in that bed over there, the one nearest the door. It depressed the hell out of me. People trying to be cheery, decorations, cards, carols, all that bollocks. That's not something you forget in a hurry. I can't believe I'm back here. I was hoping never to see the place again.'

Kesey shook her head slowly from right to left, first one way and then the other. She'd enjoyed a comparatively happy life, so unlike this girl, this victim of random circumstance, who'd drawn the short straw time and again. The detective clenched her hands into tight fists as she pictured Pearson in her mind's eye, recalling his denial, his dismissive lack of remorse. Kesey had never wanted to convict a man more. It felt strangely personal. As if the girl's future was her responsibility, and hers alone. Any form of words seemed wholly inadequate.

But she knew she had to say something. Just sitting there in pensive silence achieved nothing at all. 'That must have been truly awful for you. Not the best way to spend the holiday season.'

Sally turned away, gritting her teeth, her jaw clenched, changing the contours of her face. 'A DC David Harris made all sorts of empty promises. It was grievous bodily harm with intent. The worst kind of assault. That's what the prat said. And he was going to keep me safe. Mike would be locked up for a *very* long time. It was going to be *years*, life even, if things went well in court. That's what your pig friend told me in that oh-so insistent way of his. And I believed him too. I made a written statement. I said I'd give evidence however frightened I felt inside. And then the court gave Mike bail. They released the bastard as if he hadn't done anything at all. What the fuck was that about? Safe? Safe! I was shitting myself. The system let me down. Your lot let me down. I was in more danger than ever before.'

Kesey dropped her chin to her chest, suddenly lost for words, as the young woman continued her story, her voice repeatedly breaking with raw emotion as she relived events as if in real-time.

'I was staying at my sister's place in Glyndwr Street at the top of town. A one bedroom flat on the first floor above the off-licence. Mike came after me. He kicked the door in. And then he gave me the worst beating of my life. And he smashed the place up too. Punishment, he called it. I deserved it, apparently. My sister somehow managed to lock herself in the bathroom to dial 999 before he got in there and got hold of her too. But the bastard was long gone before you lot finally turned up. I was pissing blood for a week.'

Kesey nodded, feeling a heady mix of sympathy, anger and frustration. 'I've read the paperwork. Pearson was re-arrested, remanded, and given six months. It should have been a lot longer. I totally accept that.'

For the first time, Sally met Kesey's tired eyes and held her gaze, looking back at her with an intense fevered stare. The young woman rushed her words, her voice rising in tone and pitch, her reddened eyes flickering like a faulty bulb. 'Oh, yeah, he was given six months all right. But he was released after three. Twelve fucking weeks for kicking the crap out of me. And he'd assaulted my sister too. He smashed her right in the face, hard. He broke her nose. Twelve fucking weeks for all that and then they released the bastard for good behaviour. *Good behaviour!* He doesn't know the meaning. How do you think that went for me? It wasn't great. I'll tell you that much. It would have been better if my sister had never rung you lot at all.'

Kesey sighed. 'I'm so very sorry to hear that. It must have been truly awful for you. But it's going to be different this time.'

'Mike found me again on the first day he was out. He followed me down a backstreet after dark and dragged me back to his place. He told me he'd kill me if I ever spoke to the police again. And I believed him too. I still believe him. He's one vicious bastard. I think he's capable of almost anything. The quicker you're out of here, the happier I'll be. Because someone will tell him, they always do. He knows a lot of people in this town. They like him. He's got spies everywhere.'

Kesey bounced a knee. Her question seemed redundant, pointless in the circumstances, but she had to ask it. What other choice did she have? 'So, am I right in thinking you're not ready to make a statement?'

'Not a fucking chance.'

Kesey swallowed again, wondering why her mouth felt so very parched. She knew the system was inadequate. She knew it sometimes let victims down. But it was all she had. She had to work with it, failings and all. 'Okay, I get that. I understand where you're coming from. And I'm not going to try to pressure you into doing something you don't want to do.'

Sally's expression hardened. 'Is that it, then? Are you going to piss off and leave me alone?'

Kesey moved to the very edge of her seat, leaning forward. 'I'm not ready to give up on you quite yet.'

'What's that supposed to mean?'

'You're in control. I won't try to force you into anything you don't want to do. You've had more than enough of that in your life. But that doesn't mean I can't help you. I can ask the Crown Prosecution Service to prosecute Pearson without the need for you to appear in court. There should be more than enough evidence for a GBH charge. I can't promise you it would be successful, but there's an excellent chance, even without your direct involvement. Pearson may even plead guilty when his lawyer sees the full weight of evidence. The photographs alone would be more than enough to persuade most juries to reach a guilty verdict.'

Sally's face took on an ugly, twisted sneer as she shook her head. 'No, not a chance, don't even think about it. The bastard would make me drop the charges. And I would too. I'd do it in a heartbeat. Look at the state of me. It's too dangerous. I can't take the risk.'

The detective took a deep breath, inhaling through her nose and then slowly exhaling from her mouth for a silent count of three. 'You're not grasping what I'm telling you. I understand everything you've said, honestly, I do. I'm sure I'd feel much the same in your place. But putting pressure on you to drop the case wouldn't help Pearson at all. I can talk to the prosecuting lawyers later today. If they go for it, I can tell him he's being taken to court *despite* your wishes to the contrary. I'd make it crystal clear that it's totally beyond your control. That you've got no say in his being prosecuted, none whatsoever. And I'd do all I could to get him remanded in custody. I think it's highly likely I'd succeed given his history of violence. He could be safely banged up in the remand wing at Swansea Prison by tomorrow at the latest. How does that sound?'

Sally wiped away a tear, nodding. There was the hint of a smile on her face but it disappeared as quickly as it appeared. 'Yeah, yeah, I'll believe it when I see it. Harris was full of crap. One empty promise after another. Maybe you're the same.'

'I'm sorry if he let you down.'

'If? *Fucking if!* I don't think there's much doubt about it, is there?'

'I'll do everything I can to change your situation for the better, that's a promise. You have my word, one woman to another.'

'I don't want you coming here again.'

Kesey's disappointment was almost palpable. She'd really thought she was winning. 'Oh, come on, Sally, you could be lying there worrying unnecessarily if I don't keep you informed. I can keep in touch by phone if you'd prefer.'

'What happened to me being in control? That didn't last very long. What was it, about two minutes?'

Kesey felt inclined to argue, but she decided against. The girl had a point. 'We can do this your way, whatever's best for you.'

'You want me to talk to you on the phone? Are you winding me up? You haven't got a fucking clue. If Mike gets out, he'll check the thing. He'll go through every call. He always does.'

Kesey silently admonished herself for her lack of insight. 'Okay, so how about I provide you with a new pay-as-you-go with a few pounds credit? Pearson needn't know about it. What do you think? I could have it delivered to you today, here on the ward. All you have to do is say the word.'

Sally paused before responding. 'There's a payphone in the dayroom. I could call you from there. Although I can't see that happening. You lot are next to useless. What would be the point?'

Kesey blew the air from her mouth. 'Are you okay for cash?'

'There isn't exactly much to spend on in here.'

'I was thinking about the payphone.'

'It's not a problem. I've got my benefit money. If I decide to ring, I can.'

Kesey rose to her feet, pushing her chair aside. She handed Sally a small card with her name and the central switchboard number printed on one side in bold capitals, black on white. 'Call that number and ask for me. I had a quick word with your consultant. It'll likely be days rather than weeks before you're out of here. Have you got anywhere to go?'

Sally stared into the distance, shoulders hunched over her chest. She looked suddenly smaller, almost childlike. As if the situation had carried her back in time. 'No, there's nowhere.'

'What about your sister's place? You've stayed there before. Why not again?'

'She's got a new bloke in her life. A right miserable git who can't stand the sight of me. He threw me out the last time I slept on the sofa. He rushed me right out into the street. I didn't even have time to get dressed. I was out there in my knickers and a T-shirt until he threw my things out after me. The bastard's off his fucking head!'

Kesey pressed her lips together. 'Is there nowhere else, your parents' place, maybe?'

Sally laughed, a harsh laugh that had nothing to do with humour. 'I grew up in care from the age of six. Foster homes and then kids homes when I got a little older, one move after another. My birth parents weren't the nicest people in the world. Mum was on the game. Dad was her pimp. He'd sell her to anyone who'd pay. All that mattered was the heroin. And he never knew what to do with his hands. He didn't know whether to punch me or stroke me. Neither was great. I don't know which I hated the most. I think it was probably the stroking. I still feel his filthy hands on me sometimes when I'm alone in the dark.'

'It can't have been easy. I'm sorry you had such a hard time.'

'Oh, he was always sorry. Until he did it again. And Mum didn't give a shit. I haven't seen either of them for years. Hopefully, it will stay that way. They had fuck-all interest in me, and I feel the same about them, good fucking riddance. I thought I'd won the lottery when I first met Mike. A mature bloke, the odd spliff, a place of his own. But that all went sour pretty quickly. He didn't show his true colours until I moved in.'

Kesey searched for a satisfactory response. Something positive, something hopeful, anything to alleviate the young woman's angst even for a minute. Sometimes the suffering of others was almost too much to bear. Kesey used a line she'd used before. Something she felt she could rely on. 'We can't rewrite the past, but we can change the future. How about I talk to the hospital social worker?'

Sally looked back with a sneer. 'Is that really the best you've got?'

'Come on, Sally. It's not something you should dismiss out of hand. I've found her very helpful in other similar cases. There's always a high demand for accommodation in this part of the world. I can't guarantee she'll come up with something suitable. But she may do. Her name's Karen Hoyle, I can talk to her today if you're in agreement. Hopefully, she can help. I know she'd try her best. She always does.'

Sally turned to her side, picking up her smartphone, scrolling through the various music tracks on offer. 'Yeah, go on then. I suppose so. I had one half-decent social worker back in the day, a young bloke with a beard and glasses. Although, most of the others were shit. I may as well give this Karen a try. It's not like I've got a lot of choices. What have I got to lose?'

Kesey nodded twice, relieved Sally had finally relented. It was a small victory but a victory nonetheless. One small triumph in a sometimes insurmountable world of woe. 'Okay, that's good to hear. I'll talk to Karen before heading back to the station. I'll put her fully in the picture and stress the urgency.'

Sally placed her headphones back in her ears, humming quietly as she closed her eyes tight shut. Kesey looked back at her for one final time before finally leaving the ward, one thought after another tumbling in her mind. The unfortunate young woman had seen and experienced so very much in her short lifetime. No wonder the girl was cautious. No wonder she was scared to trust. She appeared to be drifting away, living in the moment. It sometimes suited victims to forget for a time. It seemed Sally was one of those people. And who could blame her for that?

2

The middle-aged, pencil-thin helping professional stood close to the edge of Sally's hospital bed, smiling warmly, her horsey face framed by long, curly auburn hair, which tumbled over her shoulders in a tangled web that looked as if it hadn't been brushed in years. She was holding a well-thumbed A4 notepad in one hand and a yellow plastic biro in the other. She tapped the nib of the pen against the pad three times before speaking in a singsong Welsh voice rising and falling in rhythm. 'Hello, Sally, my name's Karen Hoyle, I'm the social worker here at the hospital. Inspector Kesey asked me to call in on you. She's put me fully in the picture, as promised. Are you happy to talk to me? I want to help you if I can.'

Sally adjusted her position, first one way and then another, groaning quietly under her breath, unable to get comfortable. Her bruised ribs ached as the painkilling drugs gradually lost their power. She was hoping for the best but still fearing the worst. It didn't serve to get your hopes up, not in her world. The disappointment could be crushing.

Sally glanced out of the window as the rain began to fall, large droplets running down the pane. 'I'm being kicked out of here sometime tomorrow morning. Some doctor said they need the bed. *Like I don't!* I'll be on the streets again. It's a fucking nightmare in the summer, let alone when it's pissing down and bastard freezing. Where the fuck do I go?'

When Sally emitted a long, deep audible breath, the social worker thought it was one of the saddest sounds she'd ever heard. Hoyle pulled the pale blue privacy curtain around the bed, thinking it next to useless, but better than nothing at all. Hoyle smiled again as she sat herself down, but her tone betrayed her concern. 'You're not going to be on the streets, Sally. You've been through more than enough already without that abomination. I'm not going to let that happen.'

Sally raised herself in the bed, suddenly more animated, using her hands to support her slight nine stone frame. 'What do you mean? What are you saying? Can you talk to my consultant? Can I stay here a little longer? It's not great, but it's better than the streets.'

'That's not an option, but there is a women's domestic violence refuge here in town. It's in Curzon Street, on the hill close to the park. Do you know it?'

'Um, yeah, I think so. I know the street, maybe not the building.'

'It's a large converted Victorian terraced house intended for survivors in your circumstances – women and children in need of support and protection. I gave the manager a ring about half an hour ago. A wonderful, caring lady named Ivy Breen. She was in the same situation in which you find yourself not so very long ago. Her abuser was killed in an accident about five years since. The brakes failed on his car just before he hit a wall at sixty miles an hour. Ivy's helped a lot of women since then. Young women just like you.' Hoyle paused, a beaming smile on her angular face. 'I would never celebrate any human being's death, but I do sometimes think of the accident as karma. Such things give us hope for the future. Wouldn't you agree? Maybe there is a God after all.'

Sally's eyes widened, the whites flashing. She had no real understanding of what Hoyle had talked of, but she'd taken an instinctive liking to this unusual woman with her positive vibes. But life had taught Sally pessimism. False hope was no hope. She was very much wishing for the best but still fearing the worst. 'Can Ivy help me? What– what did she say?'

Hoyle beamed, the smile lighting up her face. 'You'll no doubt be glad to hear that a vacancy has just become available. It's a real stroke of luck. I can't stress that sufficiently. The timing really couldn't be better. It wouldn't be a long-term answer, of course. That's not how these things work. But it would at least give you a safe and secure place to stay for a time until you can find a suitable long-term alternative. What do you think? I can make the necessary arrangements if you're in agreement. Ivy knows I'm discussing the offer with you. She's awaiting my call.'

Sally's relief was evident, her shoulders slumping as her tears began to flow. She raised her open hands to her face, speaking through her fingers. 'Would I have my own room?'

Hoyle nodded enthusiastically. 'Yes, absolutely, you would. There are six women in residence at any one time, some with children. I don't know how many little ones there are, exactly. It changes from week to week. You'd have your own bedroom, with a shared bathroom, lounge and kitchen. And there are excellent security features too. As you'd expect given the building's purpose. The refuge can only be accessed via a high steel security gate with a four-number access code, which is changed regularly. And there's a panic alarm located on the wall in the hallway, linked directly to the local police station. It's a big red button. You can't miss it. If it's pressed, the police respond immediately. They're there in a matter of minutes. It's a simple, tried and tested system that works well. Ivy has developed an excellent working relationship with the other local services. That benefits the residents as well as her.'

Sally lowered her hands to her chest. 'That all sounds almost too good to be true. When can I go?'

'So, you want to accept the place?'

'Yeah, too fucking right I do. Where the hell else would I go? This is the best news I've had in ages.'

Hoyle made some hurried scribbled notes before standing. 'Right, I'll ring Ivy now and give her the good news. She'll be delighted. And I'll speak to your consultant to find out exactly what time you can leave in the morning. I'll run you to the refuge myself and make the necessary introductions. Change is never easy, even in the best of circumstances. A meet and greet should make it a little easier for you to settle in.'

Sally smiled for the first time that day, a thin, gap-toothed smile, but a smile nonetheless. She looked as happy as a much-loved child on a birthday morning. 'Thank you, Karen, thank you so very much. This was the last thing I was expecting when I woke up this morning. I can't believe my luck. You've been fucking brilliant. It's like winning the lottery. I really appreciate everything you're doing for me, really I do.'

'You're very welcome, and please don't hesitate to ring if there's anything else you need. Just contact the hospital switch-board and ask for me. They'll know where to find me. I'm never far away.'

'Okay, ta, I will.'

'You'll be allocated a community social worker in due course, someone from the adult services team here in town. But I'll keep in touch until that happens. It's a part of my role. I'll be there to support you. You won't be on your own.'

'Thanks again, that's good to know. It's great to have someone on my side for a change. It doesn't happen often.'

The social worker stopped and turned on approaching the

corridor, spinning smoothly on the ball of one foot. 'There is one thing I should probably mention before I head off. There's a no-swearing policy at the refuge. It's something Ivy's very strict on, for the benefit of the children. I hope that's not going to be a problem.'

Sally cursed crudely under her breath. 'That's not going to be an issue. I'm used to rules. I've been following them all my life.'

3

The wind was unrelenting: it drove before it sheets of icy rain that swept in off the Irish Sea, painting the Welsh countryside in an eerie grey-white hue, that made Beth shiver despite her car's relative warmth. She sat huddled in the driver's seat with the engine slowly idling, the vehicle carefully hidden from a quiet country road, on a stone-strewn side track with high hedges to either side, leading to a dairy farm on the hill beyond.

Beth checked her watch for the fourth time in under five minutes, asking herself if any man would go running on such a dank winter night, however dedicated, however obsessive, however prone to excess? But then there he was in front of her, only a few seconds late, a slave to habit, jogging up the steep incline of the hill with surprising ease, his head bowed, focusing on the road at his feet as the sleet continued to fall.

The man left her sight within seconds, seemingly oblivious to her existence as she increased the speed of the small car's wipers, preparing to follow him despite the almost irresistible inclination to switch off the engine as if she hadn't seen him at all.

But what would that achieve? She'd made a commitment. She was there for a reason. All the waiting, all the planning, the anticipation and the soul searching, had led to this precise moment in time. She'd pictured these very events in her mind's eye time and again, she'd imagined them, she'd rehearsed them, and now the time was here. There would be no going back, not now, it was far too late for that. How could she live with herself if she lost her nerve, letting everyone down at the worst possible time? Beth breathed deeply, sucking in the air and counting slowly to five as she gripped the steering wheel still tighter with clenched hands that wouldn't stop shaking. She thought she could feel her heart pounding in her throat as she manoeuvred out into the quiet road, her headlights reflecting off the back of the man's yellow, water-resistant windcheater jacket, as he continued his run one determined step after another. Beth swallowed hard, once, then again; her eyes narrowed to slits as she pressed her foot down on the accelerator, speeding towards him as he looked back, growing concern contorting his otherwise ordinary features. As if he couldn't believe what he was seeing. As if he knew what she was there to do.

Beth could see the growing fear in the man's eyes as she held her foot down, resisting the desire to hit the brake or swerve away. She gritted her teeth, jaw tightly clenched as she urged herself on: *Come on, come on, he deserves it, the bastard deserves to die.*

She continued to accelerate, thirty, thirty-five, forty miles an hour, brief seconds seeming like minutes as the man attempted to scramble up the high, icy hedge to his right. But the incline was too steep, the earth too slippery, the absence of suitable footholds insurmountable, however hard he tried to escape the vehicle rushing towards him. The man slithered back despite his every panic-stricken effort. And then there he was in front of her, at her mercy, a rabbit caught in the headlights, frozen, statue-like, getting nearer and nearer.

The car hit the man, bang, full-on and at speed, a loud thud sending him bouncing over the bonnet, crashing into the windscreen, and then tumbling onto the quiet road with dark blood pouring from a head wound as he lay twitching, one leg twisted at a seemingly impossible angle.

Beth hit the brake hard now, fighting to keep control of the car as it skidded to an eventual stop. She switched off the engine, opened the driver's door, listening intently, scanning the road with quick, darting eyes, confirming the absence of any approaching vehicles before leaving her car and walking slowly towards the man, who was moaning incoherently, more sounds than words. She stood looking down at him, nudging him with a foot, once, then again, thinking him close to death, no longer a threat to her or anyone else. But then he opened one eye, and then the other, looking up at her in the semi-darkness. His torn lips moved as if attempting to speak, but no words came, just garbled sounds that made no sense at all. Beth peered down at him for a few seconds more, feeling a confusing mix of sympathy and revulsion as she turned and walked away.

Beth was shivering uncontrollably as she slumped back into the driver's seat on autopilot, her clothes soaked down to her cotton underwear. She checked her rear-view mirror, pushed in the clutch, and then engaged the reverse gear, succeeding on the second attempt, telling herself she had no option but to finish what she'd started. She pressed down on the accelerator, not allowing herself time to change her mind, closing her eyes tight shut for just a fraction of a second as the car's passenger side rear wheel hit the man's head full-on, fracturing his skull and tearing the flesh from his face as it grated against the surface of the rough tarmac. Beth was sweating profusely despite the winter cold as she reversed on a few yards past his body, turning the headlights to the main beam with the flick of a lever and staring at his broken corpse, satisfying herself that he was dead this time, before speeding past him back in the direction of town.

Beth drove on for about five minutes, tears running down her face in a steady stream that she feared may never stop until she was old, wrung out and dry. She turned to her left, bringing the car to a sudden, skidding halt in the grounds of an ancient, dilapidated stone cottage, out of sight of the road. The sleet had eased slightly by the time she exited the vehicle. She told herself it was a good sign. A sign she'd done the right thing. That the universe was on her side. That she should continue with her plan despite her misgivings. She removed the car's fuel cap, took a red plastic petrol can from the boot, and then emptied half its contents over the seats and dashboard. She poured the remainder of the accelerant over the car's body, struck a match, sheltering the flame with her hands for what felt like an age, before finally tossing the match through an open door.

Beth staggered backwards, shaken by the sudden intensity of the blistering heat as blue-yellow flames exploded into life, leaping high into the dark sky, lighting the entire area with dancing shadows that seemed to come alive. She flung the petrol container into the blaze, then turned away, hurriedly climbing a five-bar farm gate and dropping into the adjoining field, stumbling and almost falling before finally regaining her balance. She looked back at the inferno just once before rushing away, pacing quickly over the gradually freezing ground in the direction of town.

As she trudged on, eyes focused forward, not looking back, the car's petrol tank suddenly exploded with a ferocity Beth feared couldn't fail to gain attention, however remote the area. She looked around her for non-existent prying eyes, first one way and then another, before breaking firstly into a jog and then a fevered run, panting hard, increasing her pace with each loping step towards a cluster of mature trees which offered shelter. *Come on, keep going, keep going, you can do it, girl, one step at a time.*

Beth reached up, wiping the tears from her eyes with the back of a blue-white mottled hand, as she reached the first of the trees, a tall oak bare of leaves. She paused, sucking in the cold night air, allowing the large trunk to support her weight as she rested, still panting, her chest rising and falling in a rapid rhythmic motion. She spat out a mouthful of acidic vomit as her gut twisted, her mind racing.

She'd done the right thing, hadn't she? *Of course I did. Of course I did.* She repeated it time and again as she began jogging again, already exhausted, her legs stiffening and complaining with each adrenalin-fuelled step. It was time to stop thinking. Time to still her troubled mind. She was going to need all her available energy for what came next. It was going to be a long trek home.

4

It took Beth a little under two hours, trudging through sodden fields, scrambling over icy hedgerows, slipping, falling, grazing both knees, before she reached the women's domestic abuse refuge in a quiet side street on the outskirts of Caerystwyth, close to the park. She'd avoided the main streets on reaching the small West Wales market town, collar up, head down, keen to avoid both potential witnesses and the limited number of CCTV cameras, recording images in certain public places, the town square and surrounding area. Being caught on camera was the last thing Beth wanted, however bad the weather, however dark the night, however unlikely she'd be recognised in the grainy, black and white images. Any record of her secret activities was unthinkable. That went without saying. The consequences could be dire, both for her and for others. Everything had to be kept on a strictly need-to-know basis. Secrecy was everything. Getting caught wasn't a part of the plan.

As she approached the secure, high steel gate leading to the refuge's reinforced front door, an overwhelming sense of relief swept over her like an irresistible tide, washing away her worries, aches and pains as if by magic. It was a high of sorts, a release of natural feel-good chemicals infinitely better than that engendered by any illicit drug, and in that instant, she knew that her night's work was accomplished. She'd done the right thing, a good thing, a worthy thing. That's what mattered. She'd triumphed, and lived up to her commitments, just as promised. The abusive bastard was dead, gone, but never forgotten. And the world was better for it.

She repeated it in her head, *I've done the right thing, I've done the right thing,* almost believing it. But there were still doubts. Nagging uncertainties that wouldn't let up. Thou shall not kill, the Ten Commandments. Memories of childhood Sunday school lessons; doubts that ate away at her peace of mind like a hungry dog gnawing on flesh.

Beth reached up to enter the four-number security code which opened the gate, allowing both residents and the refuge's exclusively female staff to pass. She tried once, then again, but without success. It wasn't that she couldn't recall the number, that was engrained on her psyche as if carved in tablets of stone. No, her dirty, blue-white frozen fingers were the problem. They wouldn't stop quivering as the mid-January cold continued to bite. Her entire body was trembling in her drenched, woefully inadequate clothing; the one part of the plan she hadn't properly thought through. She hadn't considered the winter sleet, the penetrating, frosty chill that had made the evening even more unpleasant than she could have imagined even in her darkest moments. Why on earth hadn't she borrowed a suitable coat, something warm, something waterproof? One of the other women would have been only too ready to help if asked. Of course, they would. They were The Sisterhood. A mutually supportive team standing up to an abrasive, male-dominated, misogynistic world. And gloves, she should have worn gloves. Leather would have been best. Blue jeans and a dark woollen jumper? The colours were okay, but, really? What the hell was she thinking? It was the middle of winter. Stupid girl! Maybe her ex was right all along. He'd said it often enough. Stupid girl! It seemed she wasn't thinking at all.

Beth tried entering the number for a third time, holding the one hand with the other to provide some stability. But a combination of increasingly numb and trembling digits made what would otherwise have been a simple task an impossibility, however hard she tried. She began quietly whimpering with growing frustration, her recent high a mere memory that now felt so long ago. She knew the doorbell was faulty. It had been for days and the promised repair not forthcoming, as the residents had hoped.

She reluctantly resorted to calling out, drawing attention to herself, the last thing she wanted in the circumstances, as she feared the potentially inquisitive eyes of nosey, interfering curtain-twitchers in the street's overlooking houses. Beth looked up, to the right and left and back again, searching for opened curtains, faces pressed against the glass, spies in the night. But it appeared her concerns were unfounded at least for the moment. It seemed the street's residents were uninterested and likely getting on with their lives. Beth looked again for one last time, searching for reassurance, her eyes darting from one building to the next, bouncing off shadows, but there was no-one to see.

She called out for a second time, more confident now, a little louder this time, and emitted a long, outward breath of relief when a light shone brightly in one of the refuge's first floor bedrooms to the left of the door. Beth smiled as a window opened, only a few inches at first, but wide enough for a young woman she recognised immediately to call out to her, barely loud enough to be heard in the street below.

The woman's tone was hushed but urgent. 'Keep the frigging noise down! How can you not know the number? It's 2163. *2163!*'

Beth looked up with haunted eyes that had seen too much,

her hypersensitive perception of the implied criticism crushing. Memories of the not so distant past flooded back, surrounding her mercilessly. And in that instant, she was back with the man who'd offered her nothing but condemnation. As if she'd never escaped his unwelcome clutches. As if she'd never left.

Beth shook herself, suddenly back in the present as the mental pictures faded. 'It's my hands. I can't stop shivering. My fingers won't work.'

Susan Johnson, a heavily made-up, twenty-nine-year-old bottle-blonde with a plunging neckline and impressive cleavage, nodded her understanding. 'Yeah, it's frigging freezing. Give me a second. I'm on my way.'

Susan, or Sue as she was more commonly known to friends and acquaintances, opened the front door a short time later, followed by the high security gate, which creaked alarmingly as it swung on its steel hinges. Sue was gently cradling a sleeping infant in her arms as she led Beth into the comparative warmth of the primrose-yellow painted hallway. Sue looked Beth up and down after closing the door, wide-eyed, lingering, not knowing whether to laugh or cry. 'What the hell happened to you? You look like a drowned rat.'

Beth held her hands out wide, fingers spread, palms faced forwards. But she didn't say anything in response. The picture told its own story. What was the point of words?

Sue's expression darkened as she spoke in a whisper. 'Is it done?'

Beth slumped to the floor, sitting on the first step of the stairs, suddenly exhausted, pushing her wet fringe away from her eyes, which were slowly filling with tears. 'Yeah, exactly as planned. I've been worrying about today for such a long time. I can't believe it's finally over.'

'Then, why the tears? Get your head up. You've done well.

You've accomplished great things. Harper's dead. It's time to celebrate.'

Beth stalled, wiping her face before speaking. Her eyes were heavy and unfocused as she stared at the floor at her feet. 'I know what you're saying. It's over. It went well. But it wasn't nearly as easy as I'd imagined it, not even close.'

'Oh, come on, Beth, don't go soft on me. Have you forgotten what we talked about before you left the house? You're a tiger. The bastard heard you roar. He had it coming. You sank in your claws.'

Beth raised her eyes for a beat before refocusing on the carpet. For a moment, the entire floor flashed red in her imagination. There was blood everywhere, getting deeper, threatening to drown her where she sat, crying. She forced the image from her mind. 'That's easy enough for you to say when you weren't there. He was human, whatever he'd done. Flesh and blood like you and me.'

Sue sighed loudly with exaggeration. '*Human?* Give me a frigging break. The man was an *animal.* No, no, he was *worse* than an animal. He sexually assaulted a little girl. A child of *four*! And he got away with it too, until today. Don't ever compare that *scum* to us.'

Beth felt her left eye twitch as her anxiety soared to a new and savage high. 'I was crapping myself, sitting there in the car with the engine running. It felt as if my heart was going to burst. He stopped running and looked back at me, caught in the headlights. As if he knew what would happen next. As if he knew that I was there to kill him. He looked so ordinary, so unthreatening, vulnerable even. Not the monster I'd created in my head. I very nearly didn't do it at all.'

Sue responded immediately, rushing her words, rocking the baby to and fro as he adjusted his position, snorting quietly in his sleep. 'But the bastard is definitely dead, yes? Please tell me you didn't back out. You actually did it, yes?'

Beth nodded once, then again, her head moving in jerks as she pictured the scene, events playing behind her eyes like the frames of a film, unwelcome, invasive, one after another. Beth recalled the dull thud as her car slammed into her target's body; the shattered windscreen, the pitch-black blood spilt on the road, staining the wet tarmac as it mingled with the melting sleet. And she heard the sickening crack of his skull as her rear wheel crushed his head, dragging his battered body several yards along the country road before she'd brought the hatch-back to a sudden juddering halt.

Beth winced as she spoke, the recent memories all too real. 'Yes, Sue, I've told you. I killed him. I didn't back out. I said I'd do it, and I did. The man's dead and he's not coming back.'

Sue swayed to the right and left, quietly humming a tune made famous by a recent TV advertising campaign, comforting her child as he woke for a second or two, before quickly returning to sleep.

'What about the car?'

Beth nodded again. 'The petrol worked a treat. The car burst into flames and exploded. I got out of there pretty quickly after that. I don't think there's going to be any evidence to find.'

Sue smiled, her face relaxing, her expression softening. 'That's good, you did well. And hopefully, anyone who heard the explosion thought it came from that military testing place near Pendine. It's only across the water, a few miles at most.'

'I was thinking the same thing.'

'Have you reported it missing?'

'What?'

'Concentrate, for fuck's sake, concentrate. The car, the frigging car! Have you rung the police?'

Beth pulled her head back, her eyes narrowing as she spoke.

'Look at the state of me.' She paused, lips pressed together, pointing to herself with a single digit. 'How would I explain this lot? Think about it. What the hell would I say?'

A look of recognition dawned on Sue's heavily made-up face. 'Fair point, enough said. We need a change of plan. You can't report the car stolen until you know it's gone, right? When you ring, you say you've just found out. But let's not leave it for too long. There's far too much at stake.'

Beth opened her mouth as if to speak, but she swallowed her words, silenced in an instant as a recently arrived ginger-haired resident in her late teens began descending the staircase, a jar of cheap instant coffee clutched tightly in one hand and a cracked red pottery mug in the other. She was holding each item as if they were the greatest treasures in the world. As if she feared someone may snatch them from her at any moment. Both Beth and Sue noticed that the girl's face was swollen as she negotiated the staircase, her many bruises changing to black and blue. Beth rose to her feet, forcing a thin smile in friendly acknowledgement as she allowed the girl to pass by.

Beth began climbing the stairs. 'I need to get out of these wet clothes. I can't stop shivering.'

The two friends entered the spacious communal first-floor bathroom in total silence. Neither said another word until they were both safely inside the white-tiled room with the door securely locked. Sue sat on the edge of the bath, one shapely leg crossed over the other, her sleeping infant rested over a shoulder, breathing through his nose, quietly snuffling.

'It may be an idea to leave reporting the car stolen until morning. It's just a thought. You could say that we spent the evening together watching telly in my room, and then we went to bed at whatever time we agree. You then went outside in the morning to head to work at the café, like you always do, and that's it, the car was gone. You searched the street, thinking you may have forgotten where it was parked, but it was nowhere to be found. Some bastard had taken it. Just stick to the basics. Don't make the story any more complicated than it needs to be. I'll give you an alibi if I'm ever asked. You know that. We're in this together.'

Beth shook her head as she began stripping off her wet clothing, throwing each sodden item to the floor one at a time. 'But what if the police turn up before I ring them? The car went up like a frigging bomb. Any number of people must have heard it however remote the area. They're not all going to put it down to the military testing. The police may have found the car by now. And if they have, there's every chance they'll confirm it belongs to me. It's all on record. It's just a call away. It's only a matter of time before they're knocking on the door.'

'What happened to there being no evidence to find?'

'My mind's all over the place. There's bound to be something. It's only a matter of time until they turn up.'

Sue nodded twice, her tone rising in pitch. 'Okay, that's fine, if it happens, it happens. It may even be to our advantage. All you'd have to say is that you parked the car in the street after work, just like you always do. And you've spent the hours since with the baby and me. As far as you were concerned, your car was sitting outside like it does every night. You hadn't given it a second's thought. Why would you? Today was no different from any other day. Just feign surprise if they turn up before morning. Force a few tears if you can. Play the victim. There's nothing to worry about. I'll back up everything you say, word for word, that's a promise. Why would they suspect anything? It's just a car theft that went horribly wrong. It's not unusual for thieves to burn out cars they've nicked. I've seen it on the Welsh news loads of times. And if the car's been involved in a fatal accident, well, that's even more reason for the thief to destroy it.'

'And if they don't turn up tonight?'

'Oh, come on, Beth, get a grip, girl. You're making this seem a lot more complicated than it needs to be. Are you working in the morning?'

Beth switched on the shower, adjusting the temperature, not too hot, not too cold, with a hand that was still trembling. 'I'm supposed to be in the café by ten.'

'Okay, so if the police don't turn up tonight, you go out into the street tomorrow morning, you pretend to be looking for the car, making it obvious, and then you ring to report it missing when you can't find it. Some bastard must have stolen it. Like I said before. That's all you'd have to say. We're not short of thieving scumbags in the area. It's no different to anywhere else. Just act as if you're totally gutted. You can manage that. Are we agreed? Please tell me you understand. You're not usually this indecisive. How many times do I need to repeat myself?'

Beth closed the shower's glass door, taking sensual pleasure in the water warming her skin. She paused and then smiled without parting her lips. 'Yeah, I've got it, either way, it's going to be fine. Thanks, Sue, you're a lifesaver.'

Sue's face suddenly paled. Her entire body tensing as her child began to cry. 'The keys, what about the frigging car keys? Please tell me you didn't leave them in the car.'

Beth spoke above the volume of the flowing water as she massaged floral-scented shampoo into her mousey, shoulder-length hair. 'You can relax, they're in my jeans. I thought I was supposed to be the paranoid one.'

Sue's relief was evident as she picked up Beth's wet clothing, shaking the jeans, reassured by the distinctive metal jingle. 'I'll put the keys in your room and throw this lot in the washing machine. Take as long as you want. I'll come to get you if the police turn up before you finish. What's more normal than a woman taking a shower? And if they're blokes, you should come out wrapped in a skimpy towel, flash a bit of leg, get their attention. It'll be a nice distraction. Let's see them concentrate after that. It works for me.'

Beth stood there, not moving an inch as the water continued to flow. For a moment she was back there on that country lane. Sitting in the car, hands on the steering wheel with a white-knuckle grip, hurtling towards a man she'd never met, let alone spoken to. Her blue eyes blinked uncontrollably. 'I'm just glad it's all over. I keep seeing his face. It's like it's imprinted on my brain forever. My cross to bear.'

'You've done well, Beth. I keep saying it. Louise is going to be so very pleased. Harper made her life a total misery. You did it for her, and for her little girl too. Can you imagine what she went through? The bastard deserved to die. We were all agreed on that, every single one of us. The verdict was one hundred per cent unanimous. Don't give Harper a second's sympathy. He doesn't deserve it. He brought nothing but misery to the world. He never cared for anyone but himself.'

Beth washed away the last of the sweet-scented soap. 'I know, I keep telling myself exactly that. I said I'd finish him, and that's precisely what I did, no more and no less. If I hadn't, he'd have gone on to hurt other women and children. Men like Harper don't change. It's who he was. It's what he was. Someone had to put an end to it. And that someone just happened to be me. What other option was there?'

Sue's reply was immediate. 'I'm only going to say this once, and you need to take it on board. There was no other option. You do not need to keep justifying yourself, not to me or anyone else. You've got nothing whatsoever to feel guilty about, not a frigging thing.'

'Is that what you really think?'

Sue nodded, feeling as sure as she sounded, starting to lose patience. 'Oh, for God's sake, *yes,* a thousand times *yes!*'

Beth didn't say anything in reply. She was still deep in reflective thought as she struggled to silence her conscience. That small but undeniable voice that still wouldn't shut up.

'Right, enough said. I'll put the kettle on. Do you fancy something to eat? A couple of pieces of toast, perhaps, or a few biscuits? I've got some nice chocolate digestives if you fancy them? I picked them up in Lidl this afternoon. The new place is a lot closer than the old one.'

Beth stepped out of the shower cubicle, taking a sizeable pink bath towel from the heated towel rail next to the sink. She began drying herself, starting with her hair before moving on to her shoulders and then her arms. She shook her head. 'I don't think I could keep anything down. I can't get his face out of my head. I can still see his eyes. He's– he's staring at me. I feel like puking.'

'You've got to try and relax, Beth. A bite to eat may help. See how you feel when you're dressed. You need to keep your strength up.'

Beth agreed, more to shut her friend up than anything else. She was increasingly tired with each minute that passed. 'Okay, maybe I can force something down.'

Sue stopped, looking back as she approached the door. 'It's going to be my turn soon. Kim's been shitting herself since the CPS dropped the case.'

'Yeah, and then you'll know exactly how I'm feeling. Talking about killing somebody is a lot easier than actually doing it. You'll find that out for yourself soon enough.'

'I'm not as sensitive as you are. Not even close.'

'Yeah, yeah, let's wait and see.'

'You worry about yourself. I can look after myself.'

Beth began towelling her legs, starting with the thighs and then moving down towards her feet. 'Have you decided how you're going to do it?'

Sue shook her head, avoiding eye contact, weighing up her options. 'I've got some ideas I need to sound out with the boss.'

'Think it through with caution. Don't just go for what seems the easiest option. I'm beginning to think using my car wasn't such a great idea. What the hell was I thinking? It leads straight back to me.'

'Nobody raised any concerns when we discussed it.'

Beth shook her head. 'Maybe they should have. I wish someone had now. Maybe then I wouldn't be so scared. I'm still crapping myself. I don't think I could stand prison. I couldn't cope with the isolation.'

'I've been in touch with Kim's abuser online. You know, dodgy dating sites, doggers, swingers, that sort of thing. I've created several false profiles, just tit, leg and arse photos, nothing that shows my face. Nothing that risks revealing my identity or location to anyone who happens to be looking.'

'I had no idea you could do that stuff. I wouldn't know where to start.'

'I studied computer science at college.'

'You've never mentioned it.'

'Garvey's into some weird shit. That's his name, Timothy Garvey. He gave me his mobile number without hesitation. I've bought a cheap pay-as-you-go for cash. It's all coming together. The twat thinks he's been talking to three different women, all of whom can't wait to get their hands on his cock. He thinks he's God's frigging gift. I've been feeding his ego. Making the prat think he's winning. When I'm ready, I can reel him in.'

'Garvey's dangerous, Sue, don't ever forget that. He'll hurt you if he gets even the slightest chance. And he'd enjoy doing it too. Kim has told me some truly horrendous stories. She opens up after a few glasses of wine. The more pain he inflicts, the harder his dick gets. It's what turns him on. It's the *only* thing that turns him on.'

'Yes, I know, the man's a freak. But maybe I can use that against him. The bastard's staying in Cardiff for a couple of weeks, fitting new shops out ready for opening. His sister told Kim all about it when she bumped into her in town a few days back. It's big money, apparently, over a grand a week. Not that Kim or the kids will see any of it. He's one selfish sod. They never do.'

Beth began drying her back, relieved to focus on Sue's future plans, anything but herself. 'Just be careful, Sue. That's all I'm saying. Think everything through *very* carefully before reaching any final conclusions. If any of us screw up, everything could come crashing down. You know that as well as I do.'

Sue moved her young child from one shoulder to the other. 'I could buy a train ticket for cash and wear a disguise. You know, a wig, make-up, dark glasses, that sort of thing. There's plenty available online. Or there's that new fancy dress place in town near the market. I could make myself unrecognisable. And Cardiff's a big place, it's anonymous. I could meet Garvey at his hotel. No-one sees what happens behind closed doors. I could kill him there.'

5

'Morning, ma'am, you look like shit.'

Detective Inspector Laura Kesey pushed a pile of crime files aside before looking up at her sergeant and grinning. His use of the term 'ma'am' never failed to make her feel a lot older than her thirty-six years. 'Thanks, Ray, you always say the nicest things.'

Lewis laughed, amused as intended. 'Fancy a coffee?'

Kesey ran a hand through her short brown hair, pushing the fringe away from her eyes and nodding. 'You know where the kettle is. I may even treat myself to a biscuit.'

Lewis made a deep sound in his throat as he bent down to retrieve the plastic kettle from the floor to the left side of Kesey's desk, next to the wall. He patted his overhanging beer belly with his free hand. 'Well, that's my exercise done for the day.'

'You need to keep your back straight. Use those stomach muscles. They must be in there somewhere.'

'Yeah, very funny, hilarious as always.'

'Take it on the chin, Ray. I can give as good as I get.'

Lewis chuckled to himself as his overburdened knees stiffened and complained. 'Late night?'

Kesey took a packet of individually wrapped chocolate biscuits from a cluttered desk drawer, sighing theatrically as she pushed one across her desk towards him. 'I was called out about 9.45pm and didn't get home again until past midnight. I couldn't get to sleep after that. You know what it's like when your mind starts racing. I was tossing and turning for most of the night. Jan was less than impressed. It's become a regular event since the force stopped paying officer ranks overtime. My hours have got ridiculous. I get called out for just about anything these days.'

'So, what happened last night? Anything I need to know about?'

'Hit and run.'

Lewis spooned instant coffee into two mugs, followed by powdered milk and boiling water, a splash of which spilt onto the office carpet. 'Why the hell did they bother you with that? Hit 'n' run's not usually a CID matter. Surely uniform could have dealt with it without you holding their hand.'

Kesey accepted her hot drink gratefully, cradling the mug with both hands. She shook her head incredulously as Lewis added three heaped spoonfuls of sugar to his coffee, before vigorously stirring. He left the spoon in his mug.

'It was a fatal on the road out of Ferryside. You know, on the steep hill in the direction of town a mile or so past the garage on the left. It was reported as a tragic accident at first. A man found collapsed on the road. Hit by a car maybe, or a van. But the traffic boys who were first on the scene thought there might be more to it.'

'Were they right?'

'Yeah, I think they very probably were. It looked as if the vehicle had hit the victim twice, once in a forward gear and then again in reverse. It seemed the victim might have been dragged back along the road for at least twenty feet if the various blood-stains are anything to go by. And it looked as if he may have tried to scramble up the hedge at one point, to try to escape the initial impact. The body was in one hell of a state, particularly his head and his face. It took me a while to recognise him. I can tell you one thing: whoever hit him wanted him dead.'

Lewis gobbled almost the entire biscuit in one greedy mouthful, washing it down with a generous slurp of overly sweet coffee as he allowed the wall to support his weight. 'Was it anyone I know?'

'Yeah, it was, as it happens, Aled Harper, the scrote with a penchant for assaulting women and children. You must remember him. He's not an easy man to forget.'

Lewis nodded his recognition. 'Oh, I knew Harper, all right. Not a nice man, and that's putting it mildly. It looks like someone dished out some of his own medicine for a change. He's ruined a lot of lives. It's about time he was on the receiving end.'

'He was only released from Swansea Prison a couple of weeks back after serving half of a nine-month stretch for breaking his wife's arm.'

'Yeah, Louise, I remember the case. Wasn't there an indecent assault allegation involving her daughter?'

'I watched the video interview. It seemed genuine enough to me, but we couldn't make it stick. It was the girl's word against his, no forensics.'

Lewis devoured what was left of his biscuit, licking the melted chocolate from his fingers as a final treat. 'Oh, for fuck's sake! Couldn't we get anything out of Harper on interview?'

'He knew the system. The smarmy git sat there saying "no comment" to every question asked for hour after hour on the advice of his solicitor.'

'I don't know how he slept nights. Or the lawyer for that matter. How can anyone defend a cunt like Harper?'

'Do you want another one of those?'

Lewis held his big hand out, palm up, fingers spread. 'Go on then, I'm starving. My alarm didn't go off. I didn't have time for breakfast.'

Kesey tossed her sergeant the packet, as his face took on a more serious expression, pensive, deep in thought. 'I nicked Harper a few times over the years. He always blamed his violence on the alcohol, like someone was forcing it down his throat. Like it somehow excused him from everything he did to the women and children who were unlucky enough to have him in their lives. It's *pathetic*! Most of his kind are the same, never taking responsibility for their shortcomings. And Harper was one of the worst, a total psycho. I'd like to have punched him in the throat.'

As Kesey sipped her coffee, she questioned the origin of the strength of Lewis' feelings before refocusing on their conversation. 'I know what you're saying. It's always someone else's fault, never theirs.'

'On a happier note, has Harper's missus heard the good news?'

Kesey smiled thinly. 'Not as yet; I did wonder if it was her driving the vehicle that hit him.'

Lewis tossed his blue plastic biscuit wrapper into a nearby wastepaper bin, resisting the impulse to cheer when it toppled in off the rim. 'I wouldn't blame her if she was. She's been a punchbag for years.'

'I've made a few phone calls. Mrs Harper moved into the women's refuge here in town very soon after her husband's release. I spoke to the manager, an Ivy Breen. Louise travelled to Scotland by train two days before her husband's death. Ivy dropped her off at the station and waved her away when the train left the platform. She's staying at her sister's place in Glasgow for a family birthday celebration. I've asked the local police to check out the facts. Better safe than sorry: you know what it's like. There's no room for assumptions in our job. But it looks as if she's got a watertight alibi. I think it's highly likely we're looking for somebody else.'

'I've known Ivy for years. We grew up on the same estate. She used to hang around with my little sister, Emily. She's a few years younger than me. If Ivy says Louise was on that train, she was on it. You can trust her completely. She's one of the best.'

Kesey nodded. 'Yeah, I met her briefly at a child protection case conference a few months back at Llanelli Hospital. The Milligan case, you must remember it?'

'Yeah, only too well, horrendous.'

'Ivy was there representing the refuge. She seemed to know what she was talking about.'

'Oh, she does, and she cares too. It's more than a job to Ivy. I think she'd do it for free if she had to. She's lived it. It's not book learning. She's not like that tosser we've got in charge with his paper qualifications and fuck-all frontline experience. She's been there, seen it, done it and got the T-shirt. There's no better knowledge than that.'

Lewis was in the process of enthusiastically unwrapping the third biscuit when Kesey's desktop phone rang out, breaking his concentration. She answered it on the second insistent ring. 'Hello, Sandra, yeah, great thanks. I'm a bit pushed for time. We'll have a chat another time. What can I do for you?'

Kesey held the phone to her face, listening to the response. 'Okay, thanks, Sandra, that's good to know. I'll get on to it.' She paused, listening for a few seconds more before speaking again. 'No, you can tell uniform to leave it to us. We could be talking murder. If Sergeant Davies doesn't like it, tell him to talk to me. He knows where to find me.'

And with that, Kesey placed the phone back on its cradle, rather more firmly than was the norm. She turned her attention back to Lewis, who was wiping chocolate from his stubbled chin with a sleeve of his jacket. Kesey made a quickly scribbled note in her police issue pocketbook before speaking. 'Okay, it's time to get serious. A burnt-out car's been found in the grounds of an empty cottage, a couple of miles from where Harper's body was discovered. I want you to check it out. And talk to scenes of crime. If it looks as if it's the vehicle we're looking for, which seems likely, I want them all over it.'

Lewis drained his mug, savouring the intense sweetness at the bottom. He swirled the rich, warm liquid around his mouth before swallowing. 'Have you got the address?'

'Talk to Sandra on the front desk, and she'll give you the details. And tell Ben Davies where to get off if he tries to stick his nose in. This one is down to us.'

'What is it with you and Davies?'

'I don't like the man.'

'You don't want to tell me more?'

Kesey shook her head. 'The man's a dinosaur who doesn't know when to keep his mouth shut. Especially when he's had a drink. Let's leave it at that.'

Lewis placed his empty mug on her desk and pulled his tie loose at the collar. 'Right, I'll be off then. You don't fancy coming with me, do you? I could tell you about a rugby trip I've got planned. I'd be glad of the company.'

'Nah, I've got to be at the mortuary for the post-mortem at ten.'

Lewis screwed up his face. 'Rather you than me. Who's doing it?'

'Dr Carter.'

'Sheila? I thought she'd retired.'

'She's agreed to stay on until they find a suitable replacement. I think she's starting to regret it now. They've had to re-advertise. It's not easy attracting consultants in this part of the world. It's been dragging on for months.'

'Well, at least you know you're in good hands.'

Kesey checked her watch and nodded. 'I'll see you later on, Ray. We can have a catch-up and compare notes. See where we are with the case.'

'What sort of time have you got in mind?'

'I'll meet you in the canteen at one o'clock sharp. I've got to be in Ammanford by half two at the latest for a meeting. Give me a ring if you think you're going to be late. I've got plenty to be getting on with. I don't want to be hanging about wasting my time.'

Lewis raised a hand to the side of his head in mock salute and curtseyed. 'Will do, ma'am, anything you say, ma'am. Your wish is my command. I'm here to serve.'

She gave him the finger, laughing as he approached the door. 'I don't know why I put up with you sometimes.'

'It's because I'm a great detective, Laura. You know that. You're lucky to have me. I'm one of the best.'

6

Dr Sheila Carter was close to completing Aled Harper's post-mortem examination by the time Kesey arrived at West Wales Hospital's brightly lit mortuary later that morning. Kesey paused at the entrance, dabbing a little menthol vapour rub under each nostril before entering the room. It was a well-established ritual, a technique she'd learnt from her much-loved mentor DI Gravel. A coping mechanism she'd used ever since but with only limited success.

'You took your time. I was beginning to wonder if you'd turn up at all.'

Kesey slowly approached the stainless steel dissection table, on which Harper's cadaver was laid out, sliced open from throat to groin. There were various internal organs to either side of the body.

'Yeah, sorry, Sheila, something came up.'

The pathologist turned Harper's head to one side, carefully studying what was left of his face for one final time, confirming conclusions she'd already reached. 'How's Jan and that little boy of yours doing? Are you all keeping well?'

Kesey dry gagged, once, then again, but she hid it well, swallowing without opening her mouth. 'We're all good thanks. Jan was struggling with that flu bug that's doing the rounds, but she's over it now. How about you? Is the health authority any nearer to finding your replacement?'

Carter glanced back and smiled. 'They're interviewing next week.'

'That must come as a relief.'

'Yes, yes, absolutely it does. And my husband is delighted too. We're planning to spend more time at our cottage in France. It's on the Brittany coast a short drive from Carnac. It's a lovely area. Much like the Welsh coast but with a somewhat warmer climate.'

'Sounds good to me.'

'Retirement can't come quickly enough. I'm not getting any younger. And there's more to life than work. I've been doing this for a very long time. It's time for a change.'

Kesey took a forward step, urging herself on, standing closer to the dissection table. She pointed towards the corpse. 'What can you tell me? Anything significant?'

'I'll have a full report with you by tomorrow morning at the latest. But I'd be happy to summarise the key points if you'd like me to. I was expecting no less.'

Kesey nodded once. 'That would be appreciated, thank you. It's always helpful to know exactly what I'm dealing with.'

The long-serving consultant pathologist refocused on Harper's body, a razor-sharp scalpel still held tightly in her left hand. 'The vehicle hit our victim front on and with considerable force causing multiple injuries, the most obvious of which is his right leg, which I believe suffered the greatest initial impact. He has a ruptured spleen, not unusual in this type of case, as I'm sure you're well aware. That in itself would have been enough to kill him given sufficient time, but it seems our driver was impatient to bring matters to a rapid conclusion. Either that or the driver wanted to ensure our man was dead.'

Kesey held her stomach as she looked on, blowing out a series of short breaths. 'Can you expand on that for me?'

Carter pointed towards Harper's head. 'The facial and cranial injuries strongly suggest that the vehicle hit our victim for a second time, the first time with him standing facing the vehicle, and then again in the opposite direction, in reverse, so to speak, fracturing the skull and tearing the flesh from his face. Here, see?'

Kesey confirmed that she could see only too well.

'The skull is fractured in three places, here, here and here. If he wasn't already dead, any one of those injuries would certainly have done it. No-one could have suffered that degree of physical trauma and lived.'

'You seem very sure.'

Carter pressed her lips together, her face tightening. 'And why wouldn't I be? The injuries speak for themselves. There's no room for ambiguity. I've told you my conclusions. If you don't like them, that's your problem, not mine. I've done my job. Now it's your turn.'

The atmosphere had undoubtedly changed. There was tension in the air. Kesey wished she hadn't commented at all. She silently admonished herself for saying too much. Sometimes thoughts were best left unspoken. 'Thank you, that's... er... that's very helpful. This was no accident. I suspected as much. But it's helpful to have it confirmed. I was thinking out loud, nothing more. I'm sorry if I offended you. It wasn't intended.'

'Not at all, Laura, I know what you detectives are like. I became rather fond of your predecessor despite his rather gruff demeanour.' She laughed. 'He often said a lot worse than you're ever likely to. I'm not entirely averse to straight-talking. In fact, I'd go as far as to say it has its advantages.'

'Grav had a way with words for sure. I still miss him terribly.'

Carter approached a white porcelain sink to her right, on the opposite wall to the entrance. She thoroughly washed both hands right up to the elbows, before calling on a diener to reconstruct the cadaver, returning the organs to the body as necessary. As Kesey nodded her greeting to a young man she'd previously met only once, she was asking herself what had drawn him to such a job, surrounded by death, dealing with a reality the vast majority would choose to avoid at almost any cost. The detective was still standing there, deep in thought, looking into the distance but seeing nothing at all, when Carter patted her on the left shoulder, smiling, revealing small nicotine-stained teeth that were at least her own.

'Sorry, I was in a world of my own.'

The pathologist smiled again, more warmly this time. 'Come on, we can chat in my office. My niece is thinking of applying to join the force. I was hoping she'd choose medicine, but it seems it's not for her. She'd value your advice. I'm very much hoping you can help.'

7

Kesey was nibbling reticently on an unappetising ham and tomato sandwich that looked well past its best when Lewis entered West Wales Police Headquarters' notoriously terrible canteen at just before one that afternoon. He ordered a large plate of three fried eggs, beans and chips before joining her at a table at the back of the room. Lewis was carrying his plate in one hand and a mug of overly sweet tea in the other.

'How did it go at the mortuary?' Lewis grinned mischievously. 'Like I need to ask. You're looking a bit green around the gills if you don't mind me saying so. You look as if you've just come off a roller coaster.'

Kesey did mind. She minded a lot. Lewis knew full well that such things were a part of the job she hated above almost all else. But she decided to let it slide. He was a wind up merchant. It didn't serve to encourage him. She pushed her plate aside, her sandwich hardly touched.

His eyes lit up. 'Oh, I'll have that if it's going to waste.'

She sipped her water, wetting her mouth, the perceived smell of death still lingering despite the menthol. 'Knock yourself out, Ray. If you want to eat yourself into an early grave that's up to you.'

He began tucking into his meal with gusto, choosing to ignore her comment, as was his custom. 'So, how did it go with Sheila?'

'I want to know how *your* morning went. Update me on what you've found out, and we'll progress from there.'

Lewis chewed and swallowed, yellow yolk running down his double chin until he wiped it away. 'Okay, you're the boss, have it your way. You'll no doubt be pleased to hear that I think we've found our vehicle. We can't be certain, not one hundred per cent. But the location, timing and circumstances make it a great bet. That's going to be as good as it gets. I can't see the SOCOs coming up with much. The car wasn't just burnt out, it was blown to fucking pieces. The petrol tank must have exploded. It's the only scenario that rationally explains the degree of damage. I'd be willing to bet the driver was keen to destroy any evidence they could before it was found. But fortunately for us, I discovered two halves of a badly singed rear number plate in a hedgerow about twenty to thirty meters from the main frame of the vehicle. Put them together, study them closely, and we have our index number.'

Kesey's eyes widened. 'Come on, Ray, spit it out, who does the car belong to?'

Lewis paused, upping Kesey's anticipation, enjoying his moment in the spotlight. It was something he did often, milking the attention of a younger but senior officer he both liked and respected. 'This is where it gets interesting.'

The DI tilted her head at a slight angle, a blank expression on her face, feigning disinterest. She knew exactly what he was doing, building to a crescendo. She tapped her watch. 'Come on, I haven't got all day, time's getting on. What have you got for me?'

He placed his knife and fork down on his empty plate, taking his time, resting his elbows on the table with his hands linked in front of him. 'The car is registered to an Elisabeth Charlotte Williams. She's a thirty-one-year-old café worker, who until recently was living in a council house in the Kidwelly area, close to the health centre. I'm sure you know it. It's just past the entrance to the sports fields.'

Kesey's brow furrowed. 'What's the particular significance of all this? I know there's something you're not telling me.'

'Doesn't the name ring a bell? Ding, ding, Elisabeth, Elisabeth Williams.'

A look of recognition suddenly dawned on Kesey's face. 'Ah, yeah, of course, Beth Williams, Beth, the domestic abuse case. Her ex got off in court. I thought he was going down for sure. I still don't know how the hell the jury got it so very wrong.'

'It happens sometimes.'

'Yeah, more's the pity.'

'Guess where our Beth's living these days.'

Kesey knew the answer long before she asked her question. 'You're not going to tell me she's staying at the same address as Louise Harper, are you?'

Lewis nodded with a fixed grin. 'That is exactly what I'm telling you. They're both residing at the Curzon Street refuge. Beth dialled 101 at twenty-past-nine this morning to report the car stolen.'

'Stranger things have happened. But it's one hell of a coincidence.'

'It's too much of a coincidence for me. I've listened to the recording of the call. Beth sounds nervous. Her voice breaks several times during the conversation.'

'It was a stressful situation. She's been through a lot. She's fragile. If her car *was* stolen, she'd be upset. So she was nervous.

You shouldn't read too much into it. It doesn't necessarily mean anything.'

Lewis made a face. 'I get your point. But it could be significant. That's all I'm saying, it could be.'

'You're too quick to jump to conclusions sometimes.'

The shake of his head was barely perceptible. 'I trust my gut.'

'Okay, I want you to interview Beth face to face as a priority. As a witness at this point, although that could change if she gives us any reason to believe she was the driver. Sheila was quite clear that the car hit Harper twice and at speed. We're talking murder. Take a full statement. Get it down on paper. Let's see what she's got to say for herself before widening the investigation.'

Lewis rose stiffly to his feet, silently cursing an arthritic knee, the result of an old rugby injury sustained in his long-gone youth. 'Leave it with me. I've got a couple of hours free this afternoon. I'll get on to it.'

'Where is she claiming the car was parked?'

'On the other side of the street from the refuge, about halfway up. It's where she leaves it every night, apparently.'

'Is there a camera outside the refuge? There often is in my experience, for obvious reasons.'

Lewis shook his head. 'I talked to Ivy. There used to be. It was fixed high on the wall to the side of the gate facing the front door. But it kept breaking down. She had it taken away in the end. The repeated repair costs were too high. The budget's an issue: the place is run on a shoestring.'

'What about the roads between Curzon Street and Ferryside? What are we talking, about eight miles? There must be a camera somewhere.'

'There is one speed camera about three miles out of town,

and that's it. I'm not sure it's even operational. The council closed the nearby school.'

'Unless the driver went through the town centre.'

He made another face. 'Nah, why would they? There's plenty of alternative routes. Why take the risk of being seen?'

'I know it's a long shot, but let's check it out anyway. You never know your luck. Ask one of the DCs to take a look. I think Tanya's free. Don't waste your own time. Focus on Beth for now. If she was driving that car, we need to know about it. Get her talking, look for any inconsistencies.'

'And if she wasn't, I guess we're going to have to find out who was. I'd give them a fucking medal if it were up to me. I'd be happy to pin it on their chest loud and proud. Harper was a destructive git. Whoever killed him has done the world a favour.'

Kesey frowned hard. 'The law's the law, Ray, we've had this conversation before. A civilised society can't have people acting as judge and jury. That's not the way things work. Think about it. It would be anarchy. You know that as well as I do.'

'Yeah, yeah, I know. You needn't say any more.'

'We're going to treat this case like we do any other, with diligence and forethought. Have I made myself clear?'

Lewis looked less than convinced when he replied in the affirmative. 'Yes, I know, message received loud and clear. We've got a job to do. I'll just have to get on with it. You can bring the lecture to a close. I know it word for word. I've heard it all before. Bending the rules is no longer acceptable in today's world.'

Kesey sighed, resigned to the inevitable. 'Keep me up to speed, yeah. Give me a ring if there's any significant developments: no surprises. Standing orders are there for a reason. They protect us in the end. We've got to follow the book.'

Lewis picked up what was left of Kesey's sandwich, stuffing it into his wide-open mouth and swallowing as he headed for the door. He called out without looking back. 'Yes, ma'am, anything you say, ma'am. If I find out anything significant, you'll be the first to know.'

Kesey doubted Lewis had taken on board a single word she'd said as she watched him leave the room. He was old-school, a dying breed, a detective who did things his way, usually to good effect, but sometimes not. He'd rarely listened before, so why start now?

8

Beth Williams was busy serving a customer when Lewis entered Merlin Lane's popular vegetarian café later that day. It was somewhere he'd never been before. An atmospheric eatery with a creative bohemian vibe that left him feeling well outside his comfort zone. Caerystwyth Rugby Club was more his scene, spit and sawdust, greasy stodge, and unlimited pints of Best Bitter on tap.

Lewis stood at the approximate centre of the room with its orange paint and multiple framed pictures by talented local artists festooning the walls, glad to finally escape the winter rain. He waited with growing impatience until Beth finally ended an animated conversation with a silver-haired woman wearing a multicoloured kaftan that looked better suited to sunnier climes.

Lewis had recognised Beth immediately. He'd seen photographs of past facial bruising, still on file. She was a survivor, one of many. The type of person he felt inclined to protect rather than pursue. A big part of him wished he could walk away. That he wasn't there at all. That he'd never found out that she owned the car that likely ended a man's life. But he had a job to do, for good or bad. If she were guilty of killing Harper, there'd be a price to pay. If she'd played any part in his death, there'd be a reckoning. Kesey had said as much. She understood. He was a police officer, an arbiter of the law. And he had to get on with what he was there to do, however reluctant he felt inside.

Lewis approached Beth as she was about to return to the serving counter at the back of the room. He got a distinct impression that she knew precisely why he was there as soon as he met her blue eyes. There was something about her demeanour that made him suspicious. He couldn't put his finger on what it was exactly, but there was definitely something. It was a gut instinct, an intuitive feeling based on hard-won experience, with no need for conscious reasoning. He trusted that feeling. It was something he'd come to rely on. Something that rarely let him down.

Lewis took his police warrant card from the inside pocket of his old tweed jacket, holding it in plain sight for a second or two before returning it whence it came. It was something he did on autopilot. Something he'd done since his early days as a detective, all those years ago. He looked much younger in the photo. Almost unrecognisable from the stout, sparsely haired, middle-aged man he'd now become. But it hardly mattered. No-one ever commented. They took it on trust. And Beth was no different. She'd barely glanced at the card at all.

'Hello, Beth. It is Beth, isn't it?'

She looked Lewis in the eye. 'Um, yes, yes it is. How can I help you?'

Lewis thought it a strange question. She'd rung, she'd dialled 101. Surely she'd have guessed why he was there long before now. 'My name is Detective Sergeant Raymond Lewis, West Wales Police. I'm sorry to bother you at work. I'm here because you reported your car stolen. Is there somewhere we can talk privately? I'd like to go over the details.'

Lewis thought he identified the flash of panic in Beth's tired eyes before she steadied herself, pulling herself together, to use the familiar local parlance. She seemed oblivious to bouncing a foot against the bare wooden floorboards as she spoke. 'Um, yes, that... er... shouldn't be a problem. The lunch rush is over. I'll ask my manager if we can use the staffroom on the first floor. Take a seat if you like. There's plenty of room. I'll be as quick as I can. I'll be back with you in a second.'

Lewis remained standing, watching as Beth disappeared into what he assumed was the café's kitchen. She returned a short time later with what the detective considered an unlikely smile on her pretty face. She met his gaze briefly but quickly looked away. When she spoke, her tone was reticent, as if she feared she may say the wrong thing. As if she wanted him gone.

Beth pulled a dark-red velvet curtain aside, pointing to a narrow wooden staircase leading to a small landing at the top. 'Do you want a cup of something before we go up? It's... er... it's no bother if you do. Although I'd like to get this over with as quickly as possible. I've only been employed here for a few weeks. I like the job. I'd like to keep it. I need to get back to work as soon as I can.'

Lewis shook his head. 'Kind of you to offer. But I haven't long had lunch. Let's get on with it, shall we? I think that's best for both of us.'

Beth began climbing the staircase with Lewis close behind, the aged wooden steps creaking under their combined weight. She led the detective into a dusty, dimly lit, cluttered room, with a faded two-seater sofa and single matching armchair located against the back wall. There were piles of well-thumbed gossip magazines on a low coffee table to the front of the seats. Beth sat in the armchair, inviting Lewis to rest his bulk on the settee.

Lewis took a statement form from his brown leather brief-case, taking his time, making her wait, before balancing his black plastic-rimmed reading glasses on the bulbous point of his fleshy nose. He pushed the magazines aside, creating space, tapping his pen against the table before speaking.

'Right then, love, before we make a start, I need to make it crystal clear that this is a murder investigation. It's become so much more than the alleged theft of your car. I suggest you bear that in mind from here on in.'

Beth pulled her head back, blue eyes wide, showing the whites, as Lewis studied her closely. He thought her reaction more than an act. She appeared either innocent or more likely shocked by his direct approach. She seemed shaken to the core. He looked her in the eye, taking the lead. 'Nothing to say for yourself, love? Now would be a good time to tell me what you're thinking.'

Beth rubbed the back of her neck, looking back at him with a pained stare. Her hand moved in jerks. 'You said– you said *murder*! I reported my car stolen, that's all, that was it. It's– it's car theft. Who's dead? What on earth are you talking about?'

Lewis stared into her face right up to the time it was no longer comfortable. He didn't like doing it. He knew it upped the pressure. But he felt he had no other choice. He stated the make and index number of Beth's car, confirming her ownership before continuing. 'I'm going to ask you a series of questions, and I need you to be honest with me. This is serious. It's not a time for playing games. Do you understand what I'm telling you?'

Beth's entire body was shaking slightly when she answered. 'Why on earth do you think I'd lie to you? My car was stolen. *That's it!* There's nothing more to say.'

'And you're sticking to that story, are you?'

'It's the truth, why wouldn't I?'

Lewis cleared his throat, coughing twice. 'Okay, if that's how you want to play it. Have it your way. I want you to tell me where and when you last saw your car.'

'I explained all that when I rang the police station.'

'Yes, I do realise that, love. I'm not new to the job. I need to hear you say it, face to face. And think very carefully before answering. Anything you say could be used in evidence at some future date.'

'*Evidence?*'

'If you ever end up in court.'

'What, have you caught the person who stole it?'

He gave her a knowing look. 'Not as yet. It's something we're looking into. But we will find out who was driving that car. It's just a matter of time. We always do.'

Beth looked close to tears now, as she gripped one hand with the other. She provided the information as requested.

'Anything you want to add?'

Beth shook her head forlornly. 'I've answered all your questions. What more do you want me to say?'

'How about the truth?'

She began crying now, a single tear running down her face and finding a home on her collar. 'Why would you ask such a thing? I'm a victim, not a criminal. My car was stolen. What on earth's going on here? I haven't even got a criminal record, nothing, not a thing. Why are you treating me so very badly? I thought I could trust the police. It seems I was wrong.'

'Your car was likely used to run down and kill a man sometime *before* you reported it stolen. A man with links to the refuge. Your vehicle was used as a murder weapon. It's my job to find the person who was driving it. As of now, I still think you're the most likely culprit.'

'You said my car was *likely* used, you definitely did. I heard you say it. That means it may not have been my car at all.'

'We've got good reason to believe that it very probably was.'

Beth shifted her weight from one buttock to the other. 'You've got this horribly wrong. I couldn't hurt a fly. If someone used my car to do such a terrible thing, it had nothing to do with me.'

'Well, if you claim you weren't driving, maybe you lent the car to somebody else. Is that what happened? Perhaps you didn't know what they were going to do with it until now.'

'That did *not* happen.'

'If you say so, love.'

Her expression hardened. 'I *do* say so. I say so because it's the *truth*. And stop calling me "love". My name isn't "*love*". It's Beth, have you got that? *Beth!*'

'Let's go over what you've told me one more time.'

She sighed. 'Is that really necessary?'

'One last time and I'll get everything down on paper.'

Beth relaxed slightly, the tension leaving her face. 'Does that mean you believe me now?'

'It's your statement. You say the words, tell your story. I'll write them down when I'm ready, and then you can sign it.'

'Do you want me to start?'

'Yeah, I'm listening.'

'All right, here goes. I... er... I parked it in Curzon Street at about a quarter to six yesterday evening after getting back from work.'

'Were you alone?'

'Yes, I'd just left work. Why wouldn't I be?'

'Calm down, love, I was only asking.'

'It's *Beth*! And I'd feel a lot calmer if you didn't seem to doubt every single word I say.'

'Did anyone see you? When you parked the car, was anyone else there?'

Beth raised a hand to touch her face. 'I suppose somebody

must have. Who knows? It's not something I've even thought about until now. Nothing had happened then. It was just an ordinary day like any other.'

'And you locked the car?'

'Um, yes, I think so, perhaps, I can't say for sure, maybe yes or maybe no.'

'Oh, come on, which was it? Yes or no? It's a simple enough question.'

Beth crossed her arms, forming a barrier. 'I was tired. It had been a long day. If I knew for sure, I'd say so. I wouldn't want to mislead you.'

'Did you leave the keys in the car?'

She relaxed slightly. That was one she could answer. 'No, they're in my room at the refuge. They're in a dressing table drawer. You can see them anytime you want to.'

Lewis raised an eyebrow. 'Okay, let's move on. What did you do next after parking and exiting the vehicle?'

Beth's agitation was becoming increasingly apparent as she wrung her hands on her lap. A thin sheen of sweat was forming on her brow as Lewis studied her with unblinking eyes. She looked as if she wanted the floor to open up to swallow her whole. But she had no option but to sit there. She knew she had to answer his questions. They both knew it. She had to hold her nerve.

'Well, I... er... I went into the refuge to make tea. It's nothing unusual. It's what I do every evening after work. I usually watch telly after that or read a book. Once I've had something to eat.'

And now a question that really mattered. 'Can anyone back up your story?'

Beth was quick to reply. 'Yes, absolutely they can. Sue and her baby were in the kitchen, making beans on toast.'

'Sue?'

'Yes, Susan, Susan Johnson, she's one of the other residents.

We ate tea at the kitchen table and then spent the rest of the evening together in her room. It's bigger than mine, and she's got a better telly.'

Lewis was glad Beth had an alibi. And he was hoping it would hold up under the inevitable scrutiny. He didn't want her life to disintegrate any more than it so obviously already had. But he had to ask his questions, one after another, however conflicted he felt in his weaker moments. There was a process to follow. And he had to follow it. 'Are you claiming you spent the entire evening together?'

'Yes, it was gone midnight by the time I went back to my own room. The baby was asleep, and we got chatting. I was glad of the company. It stops me overthinking.'

'So you're saying you were in the refuge the entire evening, yes? You didn't go back out at all?'

Beth tugged at her sleeve, pulling down a cuff. 'No, I thought I'd already made myself perfectly clear. Why do you keep asking the same questions? You don't even know with certainty that my car was used in the crime. And you've certainly got no reason to think I was involved if it was. You're treating me like a criminal, and I'm not happy about it.'

'Have you finished?'

'It needed saying.'

'Right, I need you to confirm you didn't leave the building at any point between the time you arrived back from work and the time you returned to your own room at the end of the night. Just confirm that for me. I need to hear you say it.'

'I did *not* leave the building. Is that clear enough for you?'

'Will Susan Johnson confirm your version of events?'

'Yes, *of course* she will. Why wouldn't she? It's the truth, nothing but the truth. I'm getting a little fed up of your constant insinuations.'

Lewis paused before responding. He looked into her eyes,

trying to read her thoughts. 'If she's going to confirm your story, that's good, Beth, it's very good. We all need our friends. And particularly when times are hard.'

Beth visibly stiffened. 'What's that supposed to mean?'

'I hope Sue sticks to her story, that's all I'm saying. I hope her version of events matches yours. Any discrepancies and I'll be asking you why.'

She wiped away a tear. 'It will match. It's what happened. Why wouldn't it? This is really getting tiresome. I think you're being very unfair.'

He gave her another knowing look. A part of him felt inclined to believe her but he still had his doubts. 'I think that's enough questions for today. I knew the deceased. I know the sort of man he was. But that doesn't mean it was okay for someone to kill him. The law's the law.'

'I have got no idea who you're talking about.'

Oh, she knew all right. Lewis felt sure of it. He'd rarely been more certain of anything in his life. She may or may not have been driving the car, but she knew who Harper was. She lived with his missus, women talked. Lewis poised his pen above the statement form. 'Okay, love, I've said my piece, let's move on. It's time to get everything you've told me down on paper. This is your story not mine.'

9

Susan Johnson adjusted her low-cut blouse, arching her back, pushing out her breasts, making the most of what nature had given her. She felt sure that Detective Sergeant Raymond Lewis was struggling to concentrate on whatever he was there to achieve. She reminded herself that men were such simple creatures, as predictable as night and day, thinking with their dicks. And this one was no different. He was putty in her hands. The distraction was working even better than she'd hoped. He was weak. Just a man with all the frailties that entailed. All she had to do was feign interest. Flirt with him. Keep up the act. Pull his strings. There was nothing whatsoever to worry about. She held him in the palm of her hand.

Sue smiled as she looked at Lewis across the refuge's kitchen table. She stared into his veined eyes and knew she was winning. The ageing, fat fool was doing all he could to focus on her face rather than her boobs. But he had no chance. She had him exactly where she wanted him. And that suited her just fine.

Sue fluttered her eyelids. 'So, you've never been to the refuge before?'

Lewis loosened his collar, a pink flush creeping across both cheeks. 'Well, I've been outside in the street, back in the day, before I was promoted, when I was still in uniform. Some scrote turned up here pissed out of his tiny mind, shouting his mouth off, making threats, that sort of thing. I had to sort him out.'

Sue licked her lips, first the top and then the bottom, before smiling again. 'What a big brave officer you are. I've always been unlucky with the men in my life.' She reached across the table, touching his hand. 'I wish there were more like you. I'm sure lots of women feel the same way.'

He rubbed the back of his neck. 'We... er... we really need to get on with the interview, love.'

Sue stood, approaching the countertop, teetering on her three-inch heels. 'Oh, come on, you've got time for a nice cup of tea or coffee. We're having such a lovely chat. You wouldn't want to disappoint me, would you, sergeant?'

Lewis shuffled his feet under the table. He checked his watch, making it obvious. 'I'll have a quick cup of tea, milk and three sugars.'

'Did you say *three*?'

Lewis attempted to suck in his gut with only limited success as it continued bulging over his leather belt. 'Yeah, I know it's a bit over the top.'

Sue dropped a tarnished silver teaspoon to the floor before bending easily at the waist to retrieve it, her tight skirt clinging to her curves. She could feel the detective's eyes on her, and she knew without a doubt that her strategy was working. It was time to drive home her advantage. 'It's a good thing Ivy was here to look after my little one. But I'll need to feed him soon. Breast is so much better than the bottle, wouldn't you agree? You seem like a man of the world. You don't mind, do you, officer?'

Lewis accepted his tea gratefully, clutching the cup, glad of something to do with his hands. 'Um, no, not at all, but let's get the interview done as quickly as possible. I wouldn't want to hold you up any longer than I have to.'

She returned to her seat opposite him, sitting back from the table, crossing one shapely leg over the other, her skirt rising above the knee. 'I'm delighted to help if I can. The police provide such a valuable service. I don't know where us girls would be without you. What do you need to know?'

He took a pen and statement form from his briefcase. 'What time did Beth arrive back at the refuge after work yesterday evening?'

'Oh, now let me think.'

'Take as long as you need.'

Sue confirmed Beth's story almost word for word, as Lewis continued to ask his questions, writing down the answers in a black scribbled script. Sue suspected that he'd keep asking his questions if he got the chance, probing for faults, searching for inconsistencies, sticking his nose in where it didn't belong. She was pleased to hear her baby cry in the adjoining room, thinking it an opportunity too good to miss. And so she looked down, drawing attention to the damp patches forming on the front of her white cotton blouse as milk leaked from her prominent nipples.

'Oh, no, now look what's happened. I'm so very sorry, Raymond. I really will need to feed him now. It is okay if I call you Raymond, isn't it?'

Lewis stood, his eyes bouncing from one place to the next, looking at anything but her. 'I think that's everything for today. If you sign and date the statement form, I'll be on my way.'

Sue smiled, resisting the temptation to laugh. 'Oh, that's such a shame, I was so enjoying your company. But you know where I am if you need to speak to me again. Don't be a stranger.'

Lewis held his briefcase out in front of him as he manoeuvred towards the door, one awkward step at a time. 'Thank you for your cooperation, Ms Johnson, it's appreciated. You've been most helpful.'

She smiled warmly, her overly white, cosmetically enhanced teeth contrasting dramatically with her bright-red lipstick. 'Beth is innocent, you know. You do realise that, don't you, sergeant? She was here all evening. Everything I've told you is true. Cross my heart and hope to die. She never left my company, not for a moment.'

Lewis kept walking.

Sue smiled again as she shut the steel security gate after him. She felt satisfied with her performance as she watched him stroll away with a skip in his step. She peered through the bars for a few more seconds, as he approached his car, delving into a trouser pocket for his keys. Yes, men were such simple creatures, driven by their needs and inclinations.

At least this one seemed harmless enough. Unlike some of the cruel scumbags she'd encountered over the years. The inadequate thugs who cared for no-one but themselves. But why no final comment before he left? Did he believe her? Had she gotten away with it? She sighed, pondering. Yes, he probably believed her, he seemed convinced. Or was he more complicated than he first appeared? Sue took her shoes off, still deep in thought. Oh well, she'd done her best. Only time would tell.

10

'What did the fat detective want?'

Sue settled her child on her lap while looking the older woman in the eye. 'He just wanted to check out Beth's story, that's all. You know what they're like, never taking anything on trust. I don't think he's the brightest bulb in the box. We're going to be fine. He wasn't difficult to manipulate. It's not like he found out anything useful.'

'Did you stick to the script?'

Sue sighed, forcing out the air. 'I told him precisely what we needed him to hear, no more and no less. Reasonable doubt, that's all the defence ever needs. Beth's got me in her corner. The police have got nothing. Just a stolen car that happens to belong to her. Anyone could have been driving it, anyone at all. She's not going to be prosecuted. Not if I've got anything to do with it. There's nothing whatsoever to worry about.'

'Now isn't the time to get overconfident. There's no room for complacency in our world. You know the potential consequences of being caught.'

'I know, believe me, I know. You're preaching to the

converted. I've survived this long by being careful. That's not going to change anytime soon. It's what I do.'

The older woman nodded. 'I've been thinking about Garvey. Maybe we should delay things until the police stop sniffing around. Now isn't the time to invite trouble.'

Sue looked less than persuaded as she wrinkled her nose. 'Oh, I don't know, Kim's shitting herself. Garvey's been sending anonymous messages, texts, emails, making threats, promising retribution. He's tried to kill her once, not so very long ago. And he got away with it too. He'll have gained confidence, that's inevitable. He'll think he's untouchable. There's a real chance he'll try again sometime soon. His messages are filled with hate. Maybe Kim won't be so lucky the next time.'

'Has she reported the harassment?'

Sue nodded. 'She even got her solicitor involved. But Garvey's clever, he's into computers, a bit like myself. He knows what he's doing. It's all that dark web stuff. Layers of security. The police can't prove he sent those messages.'

The older of the two women settled in an armchair, making herself comfortable. 'Then I guess it's up to us.'

'I've been playing Garvey at his own game, sending him seductive photos, nothing that could identify me, reeling him in. It's all been done with false identities and a hidden IP address. If the police ever cotton on, it's not going to be linked back to me. He'll be found dead, nobody will know who did it, and we'll be in the clear. I may even be able to make it look like a sex game that went too far. He's into some weird shit. I could use it against him.'

The older woman smiled. 'Okay, you've obviously thought this through. Maybe a delay isn't necessary after all. If anyone can get it done safely, you can. I know that. You're one of the best I've had the pleasure to work with. If it were anyone else, I wouldn't be feeling nearly as confident. I trust you, implicitly.'

Sue broke into a grin that couldn't be contained. 'Thank you, you're too kind.'

'Not at all, credit where credit's due.'

'Coming from you, that means a lot.'

'Where are you thinking of doing the deed? Have you decided on a location?'

'Garvey's staying at a cheap backstreet hotel in Cardiff. I could meet him there. It's a quiet part of the city. I'm not known there. And there's good transport links. It seems like the obvious place.'

'Yes, I can see that it has some potential advantages, but let's talk this through. Has he got his own room?'

'That's what he's told me. It was one of the first things I asked him when he suggested getting together. The moronic twat thinks he's in for a night of unbridled passion. He's not going to enjoy the experience nearly as much as he thinks.'

The older woman laughed at full volume. A full-on belly laugh that made her entire body shake. She stopped as suddenly as she started. 'Kim's moving into her new boyfriend's flat on Friday afternoon. I need you to delay Garvey's execution until after the move takes place. Kim *must* be at the new address when the police notify her of Garvey's death. That couldn't be more important. And I don't want her making any mention of this place, not a word, not a squeak. I'll spell that out when I next speak to her. The fewer links to this place, the better for all of us. We need to put the police off the scent. Smoke and mirrors, I'm sure you know what I'm saying. It shouldn't be difficult if we work together.'

'Kim's been living here for weeks. Surely the police already know that.'

The older woman frowned. 'There's no point in shining a light on it.'

'Okay, if you say so. I've waited this long. A couple more days isn't going to make much difference. Garvey's going to die. That's what matters. It's just a matter of when.'

'What do you make of the new girl?'

Sue gently stroked her sleeping child's head, running her fingers through his straw-yellow hair. 'Sally? She seems all right from the little I've seen of her. She took a right beating. At least the bruises are starting to fade.'

'Yes, but the memories may take a little longer.'

Sue nodded her agreement. It was a painful reality of which she was only too well aware. She'd experienced flashbacks resulting from her own mistreatment. Irritability, anger outbursts, poor sleep, hyper-vigilance, and a host of other problems that were only now starting to pale. She kept going for her child. Putting on a brave face. Struggling to cope day after day. The killing helped. It relieved her angst for a time. But her demons always came back. Some things were hard to forget.

'Sally seems like a child at times. As if she's much younger than her nineteen years.'

The older woman gave a sad smile. 'Survivors who've endured ongoing abuse since childhood sometimes regress to an earlier stage of development. It's something I've seen before. A defence mechanism of sorts. It doesn't surprise me at all.'

Sue touched the base of her neck. 'It didn't happen to me.'

'No, but it's happening to Sally. We're not all the same. Sally came here in fear, you with a purpose. People react in different ways. We deal with trauma as best we can.'

Sue nodded, more accepting now. 'What's happening with her abuser? Any news?'

'I had a word with my usual police contact earlier today, as it happens. Pearson's remanded in Swansea Prison pending a Crown Court date. Sally's safe for the time being; he's locked up like the beast he is. He can't do her any harm from there.'

'Except in her thoughts and nightmares.'

'We'll offer her what help we can. We can't do any more than that.'

Sue's eyes widened. 'Does that mean you're thinking of inviting her to join The Sisterhood?'

The older woman shook her head. 'No, that would be premature. I don't think we need to involve her for now. You know how our group works. It's on a strictly need-to-know basis. We need to keep it that way for obvious reasons.'

'Okay, no problem, I won't mention anything.'

'If Sally's situation changes, we can reconsider. Let's wait to see what happens. If Pearson gets off, we'll deal with him as we see appropriate.'

'Sally's just a kid. She reminds me of myself at that age, plenty of swagger but trembling inside. I'll do my best to befriend her. She could do with the support.'

'That's good, Sue, it's to your credit. I'm sure she'll benefit from your greater experience. But don't get distracted. You've got Garvey to worry about. That has to be your number one priority.'

Sue unfastened her blouse, preparing to feed her infant, who had opened his bright eyes, looking up at her with love. 'I won't forget about Garvey. There's not even the slightest chance of that happening. He's going to suffer. I've sharpened my claws. Garvey deserves everything he's about to get. The bastard has no idea of the angry storm coming his way.'

11

Kesey looked across at Janet, her best friend and partner in life, smiling as Jan continued stirring the vegetable stew she'd been preparing for the last half hour or so. 'That smells nice.'

'How's the case going?'

'Do you really want to know?'

Jan turned down the heat, allowing the casserole to continue simmering. 'I asked you, didn't I?'

'Yeah, I suppose you did.'

'Well, come on then, tell me how it's going. Ed's watching his cartoons, the food's not ready for a few minutes, we've got plenty of time to talk. You're not usually nearly so reticent to share.'

'I don't want to bore you with work stuff, that's all.'

Jan placed her hands on her hips. 'You're going to tell me sometime. You always do. Let's get it over with.'

Kesey sucked in her cheeks. 'Oh, come on, give me a break. It's been a long day. I'm not looking for an argument. That's the last thing I want.'

'Where's that coming from? I'm taking an interest, that's all. What's wrong with that? I thought it's what you wanted.'

Kesey swallowed her irritation. Forcing it back down her throat. She knew Jan had some unspoken agenda. But as hard as she tried, she couldn't work out what. 'Okay, have it your way. I'll take you at your word.'

Jan checked the rice, which was boiling on the gas hob. 'Go on then. I'm all ears.'

'Well, we know who the victim is. We know his death wasn't an accident. We've got the burnt-out car that probably killed him. But we've got no idea who was driving it. That sums it up.'

Jan turned off the heat. 'There, now don't you feel better after that? You were desperate to get it off your chest. You always are. Nothing's more important than your police work, not me, not Ed, nothing. The job always comes first.'

Kesey sighed, still unsure of what to do or say. 'How's *your* day been?'

Jan took two white porcelain plates from a kitchen cupboard on the wall to the right of the Belfast sink. 'Well, nothing as exciting as yours, of course. That goes without saying. I'm not saving the world. I'm not a superhero like you are. But I did finish painting the front bedroom while Ed was having his nap this afternoon. Someone's got to think about the house move. It's not as if you're going to do it. This place isn't going to sell itself.'

Kesey took knives and forks from the cutlery drawer. She was beginning to wish she hadn't returned home at all. 'What's really going on here, Jan? Is there something I've done to upset you?'

Jan looked very close to tears. She was holding them back but only just. 'Is there something you've forgotten?'

'Nothing that springs to mind. But there's obviously something.'

Jan began dishing up, placing the plated food on the pine table. 'You're the great detective. I'm sure you can work it out if you try hard enough.'

'What on earth are you talking about?'

'It's my birthday.'

Kesey didn't actually have her head in her hands, but she may as well have. She covered her face with her fingers before lowering them. 'Oh, shit, I am so *very* sorry. I thought it was next week.'

'Well, you thought wrong.'

Kesey went to hug her partner, but she took a backward step when Jan pulled away. 'I'll make it up to you, I promise. I'll book a table at that restaurant you like in Merlin's Lane. The Indian place with all the awards. We can book a babysitter and make an evening of it, just you and me. And I'll get you the best present ever. Something you've wanted for ages, no expense spared. Oh, I know, a night in Bath, at that hotel with the brilliant spa. You know, the one with the heated outdoor pool. We loved it there. It would be perfect, even at this time of year. Am I forgiven?'

'Don't push your luck. You're not going to be able to go away until the case is finished, anyway. You never can.'

'I've said I'm sorry. What more can I do?'

Jan left the kitchen without reply, returning moments later with Ed held in her arms. 'I don't want you to ever forget my birthday again. I've never forgotten yours and I never would. Put a reminder on your computer. That shouldn't be too much of a problem for you. You look at it often enough.'

Kesey kissed Ed's forehead and smiled. Not a particularly convincing smile but a smile nonetheless. 'I will, promise. I'll do it before bedtime. And we will go to Bath. You wait and see. I'll be looking forward to it as much as you.'

'There's a bottle of sparkling wine in the fridge if you fancy it.'

The detective relaxed slightly as the tension eased a notch. 'Of course I fancy it. We've got something to celebrate. It's not every day you turn thirty. What are you going to have, Ed, milk or juice?'

Ed looked up from his chair. 'Joose.'

The house phone rang out in the hallway as Kesey was about to fetch a carton of freshly squeezed orange juice from the fridge. 'I'd better get that.'

Jan dropped her chin to her chest. 'You could leave it.'

Kesey stiffened. 'It could be important.'

'Yes, of course, it could. It always is.'

Kesey closed the kitchen door, rushing towards the hall. She held the phone to her face, recognising her sergeant's gruff voice as soon as he spoke. 'Oh hi, Ray, you've caught me at a bad time. Can this wait?'

'Trouble in paradise?'

'It's Jan's thirtieth. I completely forgot about it. No card, no present, nothing. I'm not exactly flavour of the month, as you can imagine. You could cut the atmosphere with a knife.'

She heard Lewis laugh at the other end of the line. '*Ouch!*'

'So, can this wait or not?'

'I was just going to update you on the case, no big deal. We can do it in the morning if that suits you better. I'll be in first thing.'

Kesey blew the air from her mouth. 'No, let's carry on. I'm in the doghouse now. Another five minutes isn't going to make much difference.'

'Are you sure?'

'Yeah, let's crack on.'

'I interviewed Susan Johnson at the refuge earlier today. She's provided Beth with an alibi. They were together all evening. Or, at least, that what she claims. Either they're both lying, or Beth was telling the truth all along. Someone nicked her car. That still seems unlikely to me.'

'Where's that coming from?'

'Beth lives at the refuge. Sue lives at the refuge. And so does Harper's missus, who just happened to be in Scotland, safe and sound, when the killing took place. You know me. I don't like coincidences. I don't like them one little bit.'

'Oh, come off it, Ray, surely you're not trying to suggest there's some kind of mass female conspiracy? You're in the realms of fantasy.'

'Stranger things have happened.'

'We've got nothing to suggest anything of the kind.'

'I trust my gut.'

Kesey sighed. 'There's no room for assumptions in our line of work. We've got to follow the evidence. Just stick to the facts and leave it at that. It's good detective work that counts, not wild hypothesis.'

'Yeah, yeah, so you keep saying. I've heard it all before.'

'You are winding me *right* up. I keep saying it because I'm right. Any news on the town centre cameras?'

'There's nothing to see. Fuck all. No surprises there.'

'I think it's time for a press conference. Let's see if the public can help. I'll talk to the chief super in the morning if he deigns to give me an audience. Someone must have seen who was driving that car.'

'Are the two of you getting on any better?'

Kesey increased her grip on the phone. 'I'm not even going to dignify that with an answer. The man's a *git*! I've never known anyone so full of themselves. I wish he'd sod off back to London and ruin someone else's life.'

Lewis laughed. 'I'll take that as a *no* then.'

Kesey dragged a free hand through her hair as Jan called out from the kitchen. 'I'd better make a move, Ray. We can talk more tomorrow. I'll be in about half eight. Don't be late. It's your turn to make the coffee.'

12

Detective Chief Superintendent Nigel Halliday left Kesey waiting in a corridor for almost ten minutes before eventually inviting her to enter his unduly large office on the top floor of West Wales Police Headquarters.

Halliday was standing at the picture window, looking out over Caerystwyth town with his back to her, when Kesey entered the room. Seconds seemed like minutes until he finally turned to face her. 'I've noticed a change in the temperature. I think snow may be on the way.'

Kesey nodded. 'I spotted a few flakes when I was driving in this morning.'

'Take a seat, Laura. I've got five minutes at most. I suggest you keep whatever you have to say as brief as possible.'

Kesey's seat, as always, was lower and smaller than his. Halliday's black leather swivel chair seemed throne-like by comparison, perched as it was on a slightly raised wooden platform behind his newly acquired, overly large light-oak veneered desk. She looked up at him as he made himself comfortable, feeling nothing but disdain. 'I don't know if you're aware of it, sir, but a man known to us for domestic violence and other related offences was run over and killed sometime between 7pm and 9.15pm yesterday evening on Caerystwyth Road about two miles out of Ferryside.'

'Not much happens within the force area without me knowing about it, Laura. I'm a busy man. I haven't got all day. Please get to the point. You've wasted enough of my valuable time for one day.'

Kesey glanced at the several silver-framed academic certificates on the wall behind his chair, thinking they screamed low self-esteem. She asked herself why a man of senior rank would need such obvious ego-boosting props. She pictured him naked and stifled a laugh. *A small dick maybe?* 'Examination of the scene of death, together with the post-mortem results, strongly suggest that the victim was run over and killed deliberately. We're not dealing with an accident. This was murder.'

Halliday screwed up his face. 'I do hope you're not jumping to dubious conclusions based on limited evidence, Laura. You haven't exactly got a history of sound judgement on such matters. I sometimes think you were promoted far too soon.'

Kesey quietly seethed. And just when she thought she couldn't like him any less. Not for the first time, she silently recognised that almost everything about the man's outward behaviour and bearing annoyed her immensely. She'd disliked him on first meeting, and her initial impressions had been correct. Sometimes first impressions were spot on. 'I have the consultant pathologist's full report in my office if you'd like to read it. We're dealing with a murder case. I can say that with total confidence. The victim was hit twice; nothing else makes any sense.'

He pushed up the sleeve of his bespoke Prince of Wales check jacket, checking his high-end Swiss watch, staring at the face for a lot longer than necessary as if willing the hands to move faster. As if keen for the meeting to end. 'Murder, really, on a quiet country road in the depths of a Welsh winter? Serious violent crime is comparatively rare in this part of the world. It still seems unlikely to me.'

Kesey imagined herself kicking Halliday between his legs hard, bang, right in the balls, a mental coping tactic she'd used before. The image made her feel a little better almost immediately. 'I'm following the evidence, sir. The facts speak for themselves.'

'Your victim could have been hit by two different vehicles.'

Kesey was quick to respond. 'Yes, he could have. It's something I've considered. But the crime scene suggests otherwise.'

Halliday looked down at Kesey with the sort of sneer she'd seen before more times than she cared to count. As if she'd done something truly terrible of which she was entirely unaware. It was a look that never failed to enrage her.

'Have you located the offending vehicle? That shouldn't be too much of a problem even for you.'

She clenched and relaxed her fists while resisting the growing temptation to tell him exactly what she thought of him. Shouting out a stream of heartfelt insults would have felt so very good. 'We've both found the vehicle we believe was involved in the incident and identified the registered keeper.'

'Has he been arrested?'

Why the assumption? 'It's a *she*, and no, she reported the car stolen.'

'Before or after the event?'

Kesey brushed non-existent fluff from her navy skirt as her blood pressure soared. She raised a hand to her face as her head began to ache, pounding pressure making her wince. 'She rang 101 the next morning when she says she first discovered the car was missing. She's currently residing at the women's domestic violence refuge in Curzon Street. That's over eight miles from where her burnt-out car was found abandoned. I think it's very likely she's telling the truth.'

Halliday emitted a long, deep audible breath. 'That seems a rather premature conclusion to me. Has she at least been interviewed?'

Kesey closed her eyes for a beat, suddenly aware that damp sweat patches were forming under both her arms. She felt over-heated, sticky, in need of fresh air, maybe even a shower. Her nagging headache was getting worse. She lost focus as she looked into Halliday's face, his features becoming an impressionist blur.

'Are you all right, Laura? Do try to concentrate. You seem a little unfocused even for you.'

She took a deep intake of breath. 'Yeah, the... er... the car's registered keeper was interviewed by DS Lewis, as was another of the refuge's current residents, who provided an alibi for the time of the killing.'

'And are you satisfied with that outcome?'

'Either the car was stolen, or both women are lying.'

He shook his head slowly, looking down his nose at her as if she'd stunk out the room. 'I would have thought that was blatantly obvious to anyone with even the most basic intellect. It doesn't take a detective to work it out.'

'I'm inclined to believe the women's version of events unless new evidence emerges that proves otherwise.'

Halliday appeared more animated now, his Adam's apple bobbing as he made a strange sound in his throat. 'Well, let's hope your instincts prove correct.'

'Could I please have a glass water, sir? I'm... er... I'm not feeling particularly well all of a sudden.'

Halliday made a slight adjustment to his silk tie. 'If you're not up to the job, all you have to do is say so. It's a man's world for a reason.'

She'd never wanted to slap a person more. 'Just a glass of water and I'll be fine.'

He picked up his phone, speaking to his long-suffering secretary in the adjoining office. The middle-aged, slightly over-weight woman appeared a short time later, carrying a clear plastic cup filled with water to the halfway point. Halliday pointed towards Kesey and then waved his secretary away before she had the opportunity to speak. He waited, tapping a favourite gold fountain pen against his desk while Kesey sipped her drink. He placed the pen down and checked his watch for a second time.

'Right, do you think we could continue now? Is your little drama at an end? Or do we need to reschedule when you've had the opportunity to pull yourself together?'

Kesey felt a deep hatred for a man she already loathed. She drained her cup before responding, wondering why her head felt so much worse. 'I want to arrange a press conference for either late this afternoon or early tomorrow morning, depending on the availability of the Welsh TV news people. I want your agreement to proceed as planned. There's every reason to believe that someone will have seen whoever was driving that car, somewhere between the town and where our victim was killed. It makes sense to ask for the public's help. At this stage, I think it's our best chance of resolving matters quickly.'

'Oh, you do, do you? I've always thought it was a somewhat desperate tactic. The type of thing done by detectives who aren't nearly as good as they should be.'

Kesey still felt slightly shaky as she stood. She gripped the back of her chair, waiting for her head to clear. She was only too aware that both her patience and self-control were close to breaking point. There was a hard edge to her voice when she spoke. 'Do you want me to go ahead with the press conference or not? I don't need a lecture. Just a yes or no will suffice.'

Halliday raised a perfectly trimmed eyebrow. 'I'd take care to remember who you're talking to if I were you, inspector. I'm the head of this department and don't you ever forget it. Perhaps you'd be better suited to a desk job. There's any number of officers who'd be happy to replace you. There's plenty more where you came from.'

Kesey quickly decided that further conflict was best avoided, at least for now. Halliday's time would come, they'd have their argument, and she'd tell him exactly what she thought of him too, in unambiguous language he couldn't fail to understand. But such pleasures would have to wait. Now was not that time. 'I'm sorry, sir. I'm... er... I'm not feeling myself today. Please accept my apologies. I'd appreciate your agreement to go ahead with the press conference. It has the potential to greatly benefit my investigation.'

'I want whoever killed that man caught, and I want them caught quickly. Anything less would reflect badly on the force. And that's not something I'm prepared to tolerate. Have I made myself clear?'

'I'll do all I can, sir. I won't leave any stone unturned.'

He made that same strange noise in his throat. 'Must you always feel the need to speak in clichés? Does it reflect a lack of education on your part? A little originality wouldn't go amiss.'

Kesey's voice rose in both tone and pitch as she glared back at him, the fine hairs on her arms pressing against her sleeves. 'What is your problem? Is it a male-female thing? Is there anything about me you don't feel the need to criticise?'

Halliday walked to his office door, holding it open with a dismissive sneer that seemed to define him. 'Now would be a perfect time to stop talking. I've always wondered if you're capable of coping with the kind of pressure managerial rank entails. And today's performance hasn't exactly filled me with confidence on that score. This is your final opportunity to prove me wrong, Laura. Screw this case up, and it won't go well for you. You'll be demoted and back in uniform before you have time to blink.'

13

Karen Hoyle cradled her china mug in both hands, taking comfort in the residual heat warming her skin. She looked across the refuge's kitchen table with a friendly smile, her angular face framed by her wild tangled hair. 'I hope you don't mind me calling on you unannounced, Sally. I happened to be passing, and it seemed too good an opportunity to miss.'

Sally forced an unlikely gap-toothed grin that looked strangely out of place. 'Nah, I don't mind at all. You did me a massive favour finding me this place. I'm pleased to see you. You're the best social worker I've ever had. Even better than the bloke with a beard I had as a kid. You can come to visit me anytime you want.'

Hoyle sipped her coffee, thinking it not nearly as flavoursome or aromatic as her usual Columbian blend. 'It's very kind of you to say so. I truly appreciate your kind words. But it's all part of the service. I'm here in my professional role. How are you settling in? Is it everything you'd hoped?'

'It's all right, ta. Some of the kids are a bit on the noisy side. There's a baby that bawls its fucking head off for most of the night. But the other girls have been friendly enough. And particularly Sue: she's been fucking brilliant. She's my bestie now. She's getting us a takeaway on Friday. From the Indian place in Priory Street. I'm having chicken tikka masala with rice and bhajis. Sue's paying for it and everything, and we're going to watch a DVD in her room after we've eaten. She said I can choose the film if it's not too loud. Nothing with explosions, or anything like that. I wish I could stay here forever. It's the best place I've ever been.'

'Do you remember what I told you about Ivy's rules?'

Sally picked at a scab on the elbow of her left arm, agitating the rough protective crust until it bled. She seemed more self-conscious all of a sudden, reticent, lacking in confidence as if her previous high spirits had melted away almost to nothing. 'Yeah, sorry, I'll watch my dirty mouth. I don't know what the fuck's wrong with me sometimes. Oh, shit, sorry, there I go again.'

'Take a breath, Sally. Try to relax, and think about what you're saying before you say it out loud. I think that's best.'

Sally averted her eyes. 'Sue told me to say "frigging" when I feel like swearing. That's what she does. That way I won't get told off by Ivy. She threw a girl out a few months back. What's that about?' She laughed. 'I'm trying my best to remember, but it's a *frigging* nightmare.'

'Sue seems very nice. It's good that you've made a friend. And especially one who's giving you such good advice. I'm pleased for you.'

Sally beamed. 'I'm going to be looking after Sue's little one when she visits a friend in Cardiff soon. She trusts me. She wouldn't leave her baby with just anyone.'

Hoyle picked up her mug by its handle but didn't drink. 'Looking after a baby is a *big* responsibility. Are you sure you're okay with that?'

'Take the sprog for a ride in his pushchair, stick a milky bottle in his mouth, give him a bit of baby food when he's hungry, change his shitty nappy when he craps himself, I'll be fine. How hard can it be? Sue says I'm good with him, so I must be, she wouldn't lie. I'm a natural. I might even have one of my own one day. If I ever meet a bloke who isn't a total twat.'

Hoyle felt less than persuaded, but she decided to let it slide. There seemed little purpose in further expressing her concerns. And she could always give Ivy the heads-up. She'd keep an eye on things. 'Your injuries seem to be healing very nicely. The bruises are fading. And the swelling has definitely reduced. The hospital did a marvellous job of your nose: the break's hardly noticeable now. Have you been able to do anything about having your missing tooth replaced?'

Sally pressed her lips together. 'Such as?'

'Sorry?'

'Sue says I need an implant. You know, where they screw it into your jawbone. She checked it out online. They cost a frigging fortune, thousands. How would I ever pay for that?'

Hoyle reached down, retrieving her faux leather bag from the floor next to her chair. 'I may be able to help you on that score.'

'What?'

'Has anyone ever talked to you about the Criminal Injuries Compensation Authority?'

Sally shook her head. 'Nah, not that I can think of. I'm sure I'd remember if there's cash on offer.'

'It's a government scheme designed to compensate people who've been physically or mentally injured because they were the victim of a violent crime. I think we can safely say that that includes you.'

Sally slurped her fast-cooling coffee, a small amount of which dribbled down her chin and onto her T-shirt. 'The bastard hasn't even had his case heard yet.'

'I was under the impression that Pearson's in Swansea prison.'

Sally wiped her face with the back of one hand. 'Oh, yeah, he is. He's– he's waiting to go to Crown Court. But he hasn't actually been done for anything yet. It takes frigging ages.'

'You'll be glad to hear that that's not going to be a problem for the Criminal Injuries Compensation Authority. We can start the application process straight away. Prosecution isn't required to qualify for an award.'

Sally's expression darkened. 'I'm going to be shitting myself if the bastard gets off again.'

'You really need to try to control your anxiety, Sally. The CPS has decided to prosecute Pearson. That means their lawyers think they have an excellent chance of success. The case wouldn't be happening otherwise. Try to take comfort in that.'

'Yeah, but what if they screw it up?'

The social worker looked back at Sally with genuine empathy. The young survivor's angst was so desperately apparent despite her best efforts to hide it from the world. There was a sadness about Sally. Life had beaten her down so very badly. No silver spoon for her, just disadvantage and the cycle of deprivation that followed her like a dark shadow hiding from the light.

'Try to stay positive if you can. There's no reason to think the case won't go well. The local CPS has an excellent reputation. I know the man in charge personally. He's one of the good guys.'

'Sue says the system sucks. Sometimes we have to keep ourselves safe. We can't rely on anybody else. Sometimes it's down to us girls.'

'Do you know what she meant by that?'

Sally touched the base of her neck. 'No, I don't, not really, Sue's cleverer than me.'

Hoyle took a notepad and pen from her bag. 'How about I ask you a few pertinent questions, and we start the application process? Ivy mentioned that you struggle a little with your reading and writing. But not to worry. I can complete the paperwork for you, if you like. What do you think? Shall we go for it?'

Sally had no idea what 'pertinent' meant, but she got the gist. 'Um, yeah, I guess so, that would be great. A few quid's always welcome. I could buy a big telly for my room, oh, and a new computer, one of the good ones. I could go on Facebook and that, like I do on my phone. I've sent Sue a friend request.'

'Don't forget about your dental work.'

Sally raised a hand to her face, fingering the space where her tooth had so recently been. 'I look like a twat. I feel like shit every time I look in the mirror. How could I possibly forget about that?'

The two women spent the next twenty minutes or so talking through the events that had led Sally to the refuge door. Hoyle made notes as necessary, clarifying critical points before writing them down. 'Okay, I think I've got everything I'm going to need. Is there anything you'd like to ask me before we finish?'

'Um, no, I don't think so. I'm surprised I'm getting anything at all. Sue is going to be well chuffed when I tell her. We could throw a party to celebrate. I'll have to ask Ivy if it's okay. But she won't mind. Although we can't get pissed. It's one of the rules, no drunkenness. I can't wait.'

Hoyle stood and reached for her olive-green woollen coat, a birthday gift, which was hanging over the back of her chair. 'Ivy mentioned that you haven't been outside the refuge since your arrival, not even once. I'm about to have a quick walk in the park before heading back to the hospital. Do you fancy coming with me? It would do you good if you could.'

Sally's face paled. She looked almost ghostlike in the light of the electric bulb. 'I don't think so. Every bloke I see looks like Mike. I know it doesn't make any sense. But that's the way it is. It scares the shit out of me.'

'Come on, I'll stay close. You can't stay cooped up in here forever.'

Sally gripped the edge of the table with both hands. 'My ribs are still hurting where he kicked me. I don't think I could get as far as the park. Maybe in a week or two, I'll be better then.'

'How about I drive us as far as the entrance to the park in my car, and we walk from there? The rain has stopped, and it's not nearly as cold as it's been. We'll have a quick stroll, and then I'll run you back here as soon as you're ready. How does that sound? It will take us twenty minutes, maybe half an hour at most.'

'Do you– do you really think it would be okay?'

Hoyle placed an open hand on each of Sally's shoulders, smiling. 'It's just a walk in the winter sunshine. Pearson's locked up in Swansea, and I'll be with you the entire time. There's nothing to worry about.'

Sally took a backward step. 'Do you promise you'll– you'll stay close to me the whole time? You won't ever leave me on my own?'

Hoyle looked into Sally's haunted eyes and nodded. 'If it means that much to you, then yes, I promise, I'll stay close. You have my word. Do this the once, and it will be much easier the next time. You can look forward to a better, more confident future. You deserve that after everything you've been through. You will feel stronger given time. Nothing lasts forever, not even this.'

Sally began rubbing her wrist with restless fingers. 'Everything in my life always turns to shit.'

'That's not going to happen this time. Your injuries are healing well, your abuser is locked up in a cell, we're applying for financial compensation, and you've made a nice new friend. There's a lot of good things happening in your life. Try to focus on that.'

Sally's expression softened. 'Sue will be back from the shops soon. She'll be surprised if I've been out. She says I'm a tiger, not a mouse. I could tell her all about our walk.'

Hoyle took her car keys from her bag, holding them loosely by the fob. 'That's the spirit. Come on, let's get going. You'll be back here nice and snug in the warm before you know it. Sue will be so very proud of you.'

Sally fetched her quilted charity shop coat from her room before meeting Hoyle in the primrose hallway. Sally still appeared nervous. But there was an excitement too. 'Are you– are you going to be my social worker from now on?'

'Have you still not heard anything from the adult services team here in town?'

Sally shook her head. 'Not a fucking thing.'

Hoyle gave her a disapproving look. 'It's a busy time of year. Maybe we can stretch the rules. I'll have a word with the team manager to see if she's happy for me to continue seeing you for the foreseeable future. I can't see there being a problem.'

Sally looked suddenly younger, as if the years of torment had melted away. She pointed to a small screen on the wall at eye level to the side of the front door close to the bright-red panic button. 'You can see who's outside with this. Look, you press this, see?'

Hoyle smiled, nodded, and then opened the front door, squinting slightly when the winter sunshine caught her face. She could feel Sally trembling as she took her hand, leading her through the security gate and out into the quiet street. 'There you go, you've done it. Onwards and upwards, it will be easier from here on in. Sometimes the fear of doing something is far worse than actually doing it.'

Sally appeared close to losing control as she looked to the left and right, but she somehow held it together. 'Which car is yours?'

'It's the white convertible over there behind the silver Mercedes.'

'That is *seriously* cool. Can we take the roof off?'

Hoyle was surprised to find Sally still holding her hand as they crossed the road towards the vehicle. 'It's a bit chilly for that, don't you think?'

'Oh, come on, please, please can we? I'll do my coat up. My hood's got fur on. I don't mind the cold. It's not as if it's raining or anything.'

'Well, maybe just for a minute or two. As a reward for you being so brave.'

Sally sat in the passenger seat, wincing slightly as she fastened her seat belt. 'I hope Sue sees me sitting here, looking like a princess.'

Hoyle started the powerful engine with a single turn of the key. It was a good sound, a reassuring sound that pleased her. 'It seems you two have become close.'

'Sue's like my new mum, a proper mum, not like the shit one I had as a kid.'

'Do you still want me to take the roof off?'

Sally gave a little cheer. 'Yeah, let's go for it.' She made a low growling sound deep in her throat and laughed, holding her hands out in front of her, as if her fingers were slowly turning an invisible dial. 'I'm a tiger, look at my claws.' She made the same snarling sound again, a little louder this time, more full of herself as if gaining confidence. 'I'm a tiger, a powerful tiger. That's what Sue says. The world should hear me roar.'

14

Aled Harper's grieving mother stood in the faded hallway of her three bedroom semi-detached Caerystwyth council house, staring into a recently inherited Victorian mirror that had once belonged to her maternal grandmother. Renee Harper asked herself where all the years had gone. Time had passed so very quickly. She looked older, her hopes were dashed, and the future seemed to hold little, if any, promise.

Renee adjusted her permed, dyed black hair as she waited for Kesey's arrival, all the time asking herself what the point of such vanities was. Her home was empty, and nobody cared. She felt invisible as if she didn't matter at all. Was leaving the house such a good idea? To appear in public. To appear on camera for all to see. Was there any point in anything at all anymore? Surely the police could conduct the press conference without her involvement. It was their job to find her son's killer, not hers. Was that too much to ask?

Renee took a brandy bottle in hand. She unscrewed the cap and raised the spirit to her mouth, keen to seek the mind-numbing oblivion it offered. She was seriously considering returning to bed to hide from the world when a car horn beeping twice in the street outside made her grip the bottle still tighter. *Oh, God, this is it. The time has come. One more swig, yes one more swig.* And then open the front door. Perhaps seeking peace of mind wasn't such a bad idea, after all. Best get it over with as quickly as possible.

Renee walked down her concrete path towards Kesey's parked car with the demeanour of a convicted felon approaching the gallows. She forced a smile when the detective left the vehicle to greet her. But Renee wasn't fooling anybody, least of all herself. Kesey attempted conversation during the journey, but Renee wasn't in the mood to talk. The two women sat in virtual silence until they pulled up in the West Wales Police Headquarter car park about twenty minutes later. Renee was glad to get out of the car. The quicker the day was over, the happier she'd be.

Despite her best efforts to dress to impress, Renee felt old and jaded as the two women crossed the car park in the direction of the building's entrance. She'd been the only one of her son's relatives to agree to attend the press conference, and even she'd been reluctant until persuaded. Aled's father had refused point-blank, as had his sister, who'd announced through a flood to tears that she was glad her brother was dead. They'd both told Renee of their refusal to her face. As if her feelings didn't matter in the slightest. As if they didn't care. Renee asked herself if she should have done the same as she followed Kesey up the steps into the reception area. Should she have ignored the inspector's persuasive arguments? No, a mother was loyal to the end.

Renee took a deep breath now and planted her feet for fear of collapsing. Her legs felt weak. As if they may cave in under her at any second, as they had once before when she was first told of her son's sudden death. Renee so wanted to turn and run. To get out of there. To be somewhere else entirely, somewhere far away. But that wasn't an option. Not if she wanted her son's killer found. If a press conference helped facilitate that end, she had to take part, however unwilling she felt inside. And so she'd had her hair done, she'd bought a new two-piece suit from a shop she'd never previously visited, for a price she couldn't afford. And she'd drunk almost a quarter of a bottle of Spanish brandy, a souvenir of the Costas, before leaving the house that morning. Liquid courage when she needed it most.

As broken-hearted as Renee undoubtedly felt, a small part of her wasn't mourning her son's death with the intensity she'd expected as the two women made their way through the modernist building. Renee felt conflicted. Maybe her son had it coming. Those who lived by the sword often died by it too. Wasn't that how the saying went?

Yes, she'd do all she could to help find her son's killer. She owed him that much. That was her duty as a mother. She'd both pay for and attend his funeral, and she'd pray for his soul. But then life would go on, for good or bad. Renee hoped that one day she may understand what made her son the man he'd become. The man she loved but whose behaviour she hated with a burning strength that was so hard to bear. She thought of that now as they approached the conference room. One day she may make sense of it all. But for now, she just wanted to get through the morning without breaking down completely. She didn't want to make a complete fool of herself for all to see. Not here, not now, not in front of all those people, strangers, none of who knew what troubles her life had entailed.

Renee Harper preferred to do her crying in private when no one but God could see. She had to stay strong. Now wasn't a time for weeping. That would come later.

Kesey pushed open the conference room's large double doors, entering first with Renee close behind. They were met by what felt like a bombardment of flashing cameras and rowdy journalistic jabber, the attendant members of the press keen for the next attention-grabbing front-page article.

The two women stopped, steadying themselves, gaining their bearings before sitting behind a white cloth topped table at the front of the room, directly in front of a large West Wales Police logo. Lewis, who was already seated, nodded his greeting. Renee had met him once before in the days when she was still in denial. Unwilling or unable to accept the reality of her son's capacity for ruinous evil. But that had changed long ago. All her fight was gone. Renee knew Lewis could see it in her face. It was as clear as a large-print book. She took no comfort in the sergeant's welcome as she sat back and waited. It engendered no fond memories. Nothing that put her at ease. She'd never felt more uncomfortable or embarrassed as she looked out on the assembled crowd. But she felt a determination too. Soon it would be over and hooray to that.

15

Kesey checked her watch, a recent Christmas gift from Jan, watching the seconds tick by until the press conference's scheduled start time. The detective looked out on the two rows of seated journalists, some with cameras, all with notepads, and raised a hand to silence them, half expecting them to continue talking. But all was quiet in a moment as Kesey stood at the front of the room and spoke, the hint of a west Wales accent merging with her Midlands vocal sounds. When she uttered her first sentence, the words were familiar and delivered on autopilot without the need for preparation or rehearsal. She'd attended more press conferences than she cared to count. She'd led several in recent months. Why make work for herself? There was little point in reinventing the wheel.

Kesey glanced from one journalist to the next, recognising several she'd met before in similar circumstances. Some she was pleased to see and others not so much. 'Good morning, everyone, it's time to make a start. I'll begin by welcoming you all to West Wales Police Headquarters. Thank you all for coming. I hope we have a productive time. For anyone who doesn't know me, my name is Detective Inspector Laura Kesey, the lead officer, or senior investigating officer for the case we're here to discuss.'

She paused, collecting her thoughts, and then turned to point at Lewis, who had a blank look of disinterest on his recently shaved face. 'I'd like to introduce you, firstly to Detective Sergeant Raymond Lewis, my second-in-command, who is seated to my left, and to Mrs Renee Harper, the victim's mother, who, as you can see, is seated to my right. I plan to update you all on the case and then allow time for any questions at the end of my presentation. I have to say, however, that there may be some issues on which I'm unable to comment at this time.'

Kesey waited for what she considered the unavoidable whispers of dissatisfaction to evaporate before speaking again, louder this time, insisting on being heard. 'As most of you are already aware, thirty-four-year-old Mr Aled Harper was run over and killed on Caerystwyth Road, a short distance from Ferryside, sometime between 7pm and 9.15pm on the nineteenth of this month. Forensic evaluations of both the scene of death and of the victim's body have clearly established that we are dealing with a crime of violence rather than a tragic accident as was first suspected.'

Kesey silently cursed as a casually dressed local journalist seated in the front row raised a hand in the air. Kesey knew the man of old. And knew the look on her face must have told its own story. She didn't like him or his inevitable criticisms one little bit.

Kesey glared at the journalist, waiting for him to speak, fearing the worst.

'How could you possibly know that it's not an accident? Mr Harper was hit by a vehicle on a dark country road with poor visibility. It was sleeting that night. The road is narrow and unlit. That seems like an accident waiting to happen.'

Kesey took a forward step, positioning herself directly in

front of the offending journalist, almost at touching distance. Her frustration was obvious to anyone who cared to look. 'We have officers expert in evaluating both the scenes of crimes and traffic accidents. The evidence gathered in this case, is emphatic. As were the findings of the post-mortem examination, which was performed by the most senior and experienced pathologist in the county. We're not here to discuss the nature of the incident. We've already established that we're dealing with a murder. I intend to share what details I can without compromising the integrity of the investigation. Please allow me to continue. I would ask that any further questions are delayed until the conclusion of my talk.'

No-one said a word.

Kesey turned, looking at Lewis, who was attempting to mask a grin with only partial success. 'Switch the laptop on now, please, Ray. It's time for the first slide.'

Lewis flicked a switch, projecting a sizeable six-by-four-foot colour photo of a bright red Ford Fiesta on the white-painted wall to the side of the force logo. Kesey looked around the room, weighing up the photo's impact. The journalists seemed interested. It appeared the picture had had the desired effect.

'This isn't a photograph of the actual car we believe was driven by the perpetrator. But it is the same make, colour and model.' Kesey waited for a few seconds before speaking again, allowing the journalists to make their written notes.

'If you could display the second slide now, please, Ray.'

Lewis followed instructions quickly and efficiently.

'What you see now is the index number of the actual car that we strongly suspect hit Aled Harper that evening. The vehicle was reported stolen a few hours after the fatal incident. While we are following several important leads, as of now we don't know who was driving the car at the time of Mr Harper's death.'

'Whose car is it?'

'Who owns the car?'

'Is an arrest likely anytime soon?'

'What more can you tell us?'

Kesey ignored the barrage of questions, fired from different parts of the room. Instead, she looked directly into the Welsh TV news camera, clearly articulating each word. 'I'm appealing to any members of the public to contact the police as a matter of urgency if they saw the car described at any time after 5.30pm on the nineteenth of this month.'

Kesey nodded to Lewis and then pointed to a phone number projected on the wall by the last slide. 'Anyone with any relevant information should ring this number to speak directly to one of my team, who will be waiting for your calls. You can contact us twenty-four hours a day, seven days a week. As I said, please don't hesitate to call if you either saw the car or have any other information which may be relevant to our investigation.'

Kesey turned away from the camera, returning to her original position. 'Now, are there any final questions before I ask Mrs Harper to share anything she wishes to say.'

Kesey waited for about thirty-seconds of silence before finally inviting Renee Harper to address the room. 'If you'd like to speak, Mrs Harper, now would be a good time.'

Renee cleared her throat as she stood, her hands resting heavily on the table in front of her. As she spoke there was no hiding her distress. It was plain for all to see. 'My s-son wasn't a good man. And some w-would say he was a bad man. Some may even think that he d-deserved to die that night. Or that the world is better off without him. But he was my b-boy. And I'll miss him despite his many failings. I'm begging anyone who knows who k-killed Aled to contact the police. Not for his sake but for mine. Perhaps then I'll be able to s-sleep again instead of lying awake all night with my mind racing until morning. Have mercy on a grieving mother. That's all I'm asking. Maybe the t-truth will help still my anxious mind. Soon I'll bury my wayward son. I need to know who sent him to his grave.'

Renee was about to sit herself back down when her legs gave way under her. A jolt of pain exploded in her chest and fired down one arm as the room went blank. Kesey was already calling for an ambulance when Renee hit the floor hard, her head bouncing off the carpet. Lewis performed CPR, panting to the beat of a disco classic for a full ten minutes until two paramedics finally burst into the room.

The journalists had their story up close and personal.

Renee Harper's troubles were over. She was declared dead on arrival at West Wales General Hospital.

16

Lewis met Kesey's gaze and frowned. 'Well, that went well.'

'Yeah, thanks very much for that, Ray. I could do without the sarcasm. It's already been a shit day without you making it worse.'

'The poor cow was only fifty-eight years old. That's only a year older than I am. It makes you think.'

Kesey blew the air from her mouth with an audible whistle. 'How do you think the conference went, obvious disasters apart? Do you think it will get us anywhere?'

Lewis rested his weight on the edge of Kesey's desk with his legs spread wide. 'Let's hope so. We've got fuck-all else at the moment.'

'I had a word with the BBC Wales news people after everything went quiet. They're going to feature the case on this evening's programme. Obviously, they're going to talk about Renee, there's no avoiding that given what happened. But they'll talk about the car too. Our request for information will be prominent. They've guaranteed me that. They want to help.'

'I thought you'd be making an appearance.'

'I did offer, but they said they've got all they need.'

'Fancy a coffee?'

Kesey shook her head. 'I was just about to head down to the canteen for a quick sandwich. Are you going to join me?'

Lewis followed Kesey into the corridor and towards the lift at the end. 'Did she have a history of heart problems?'

Kesey shrugged. 'Renee? How would I know? She was under a lot of pressure. The stress must have been horrendous. That's enough to kill some people. Maybe it did for her.'

Lewis squeezed into the lift alongside his boss. 'Perhaps it's time for me to lose a bit of weight. My dad died of a heart attack in his early seventies. I don't want to be the next one.'

'When did you last have a medical?'

'It's been a while.'

'Maybe it's time.'

Lewis nodded. 'Yeah, maybe, I'll give it some thought.'

The two officers walked into the canteen, Lewis now taking the lead. Kesey looked at him incredulously when he ordered his usual egg, beans and chips with a smile. 'You had me going for a moment there. I actually thought you were serious.'

'I'm cutting down from three sugars to two. Everyone's got to start somewhere. There's no point in overdoing things, that's stressful in itself.'

Kesey ordered a prawn and mayo sandwich before sitting herself down. Lewis joined her minutes later with his plated food in hand.

'Just as I like it, nice 'n' greasy. A bit of brown sauce and it'll be perfect.'

'What more can I say, Ray. I've tried telling you. Have you ever thought about eating a salad?'

'Do I look like a rabbit?'

She gave him a reproachful look. 'I've got to leave early today. It's a family thing. Give me a ring if we get any useful information, yeah? The Welsh BBC news starts at half six. Hopefully, we'll get some calls soon after that.'

'Let's hope so. We could do with a break. Short of re-interviewing Beth and Sue, I don't know where else we can go. It's all dead ends.'

'I can't see that achieving anything. Let's just see who rings in. A lot of people watch the programme. Someone will have seen something. They always do.'

Lewis finished eating, pushing his plate aside before draining his mug and standing.

'My God, Ray, that didn't touch the sides. You need to slow down. I've never known anyone eat so fast.'

'I'll see you later, boss. If we get anything useful, you'll be the first to know.'

'I said much the same thing to Halliday.'

'Maybe tonight we'll hit the jackpot. There's not much more to say.'

17

Kesey was ploughing through piles of unwelcome paperwork, a part of the job she didn't particularly enjoy, when her office phone rang out at just after ten that morning. She swallowed her second chocolate truffle of the day, picked up the handset, and held it to her face after the third insistent ring.

'Morning, Sandra, yeah, good thanks. How are things with you?'

Kesey listened to the reply with only a passing interest. She checked the time. 'That's great, I'm glad you're feeling better. I've got a load of stuff to do. I'd better get on. What have you got for me?'

The inspector listened as Sandra told her that a Captain Geoffrey Smyth-Brown had called at the police station asking to see the detective in charge of the Harper case.

All of a sudden Kesey was on full alert. This could be it. This could be what they were waiting for. A break to crack the case. 'Is he there now?'

Sandra confirmed that he was.

'Okay, that's good. This could be important. Put him in

whichever interview room's free and make certain he doesn't leave until after I've seen him. Make him a hot drink if it helps. And tell him I'm on my way. I'll be down within two minutes.'

Kesey heard Sandra talking to the witness at the other end of the line before placing the handset back on its cradle. The detective was aware of her anticipation rising as she rose to her feet. She had the hint of a smile on her face as she popped a third chocolate truffle into her mouth and headed towards the lift.

Kesey entered interview room one to be met by a slim, smartly dressed man in his mid- to late-seventies, who stood and offered his hand in greeting as she approached him. She quickly decided that his double-barrel surname, grey slacks, crisp white shirt, old-school tie, dark-blue blazer and slicked down hair parted to one side, suggested his membership of the monied middle classes.

'Inspector Kesey, I presume?'

Kesey shook his hand, not too firmly but not too limply either. 'Yes, that's right, Laura Kesey, and Laura will be fine. You're here as a witness: there's no need for formality.'

'And you can call me Geoffrey. I very much hope I'm not wasting your time.'

Kesey was hoping the same thing. 'Take a seat, please, captain. Make yourself comfortable, and we'll make a start.'

He sat a little stiffly as if his back were giving him problems despite his relatively sprightly appearance. 'Am I correct in thinking that you're the young lady in charge of the Harper case?'

Kesey sat opposite him, separated only by a small table, and nodded. 'Yes, that's right, I'm the lead officer. What can you tell me? I'm very much hoping you can help.'

Smyth-Brown adjusted his position, shifting in his chair. He took a brown plastic medicine bottle from an inside pocket of his blazer, popping a single pill into his open mouth and swallowing, washing it down with a slurp of tea before speaking again. He was clearly in no hurry. There was a confidence about him, a self-assurance. As if he were comfortable in his own skin. 'I saw the report on the Welsh evening news. I usually watch the programme. It's good to keep up with local events, wouldn't you agree? I think I may have seen the red Fiesta that was mentioned. It seemed advisable to tell you.'

Kesey moved to the edge of her seat. 'When and where?'

He smiled without parting his lips. 'Ah, yes, I thought that may interest you.'

Kesey's irritation was betrayed by her expression. 'I'd be grateful if you'd answer my question.'

'I'd just left the large Tesco store here in town at approximately twenty-hundred hours on the nineteenth of this month. The Fiesta passed by as I was sitting at the junction waiting for the traffic lights to change. It was thirty, maybe forty feet away from me at most.'

Kesey took a statement form from a drawer below the table. She had no particular reason to doubt her witness. But she had to be sure of his reliability. Experience had taught her to be cautious. It was surprising how many people made false statements in such circumstances, just for the attention it brought. Others were just plain wrong. 'That seems very specific if you don't mind me saying so. Why would that particular car stick in your mind?'

The captain broke into a smile that lit up his face. He looked suddenly younger, his shoulders straight and back. 'Ah, yes, I thought you may ask me that. I spent some time in military intelligence as a young man. In the Far East in the main, although I spent some time in Aden too. I would have asked the exact same thing.'

Kesey admonished herself for her earlier impatience. 'So, what's the answer?'

'A rather attractive lady friend of mine had a very similar car some years ago. It was an earlier model back then of course. But not so very different to look at. I thought of her as the car passed on by. Such a lovely girl, I'd love to see her again.'

Kesey didn't have time for reminiscences, however well-intentioned or fondly recalled. 'What direction was the car travelling in when you saw it that evening?'

'It was heading out of town. I can say that with absolute certainty. There's no doubt in my mind.'

Kesey knew it was a long shot, but she asked anyway. 'Did you see the index number?'

He looked crestfallen. 'No, I'm afraid not. It's not something I even thought about. Why would I? I couldn't possibly have known it would become important.'

'Could you make an estimate of the age of the car for me?'

'No, I really don't think I could. I wouldn't want to guess. I'm fond of Ford. I've owned several myself. But I'm no expert. The last thing I'd want to do is mislead you.'

Kesey frowned hard. 'So, it may not have been the car we're interested in.'

'No, but it could be. Isn't that the point, my dear? It could be.'

He was correct, of course. It was a potential lead that couldn't be ignored. 'I want you to think very carefully before answering my next question.'

'Very well, I'm listening. I'll do my very best to assist you if I can.'

'Did you see the driver?'

He nodded reticently. 'Yes, I believe so. My night vision isn't what it was. But I've been giving it a great deal of thought since seeing your appeal. I've been trying to picture the scene in my mind.'

'So, what can you tell me?'

'I can't be entirely certain, I couldn't guarantee it, but I believe a brown-haired man was in the driver's seat. I couldn't tell you his age or give a meaningful description other than the hair, but I am fairly sure the driver was male.'

Kesey was quick to respond. 'You used the words "fairly sure". Put a percentage on it for me.'

He looked into the distance as if travelling back in time. 'Oh, let me think, I'd say I'm seventy, maybe eighty per cent sure. I'm sorry I can't be more certain than that. I'm afraid it's the best I can do.'

'Was there anyone else in the car?'

'No, the driver was alone. I've no doubt on that score.'

Kesey made some scribbled notes in her pocketbook rather than prepare a formal written statement. It wasn't exactly what she'd hoped for, but it was better than nothing. She pushed an A4 sheet of paper and pen across the table. 'If you could write your full name, address, and contact details down for me, that would be helpful.'

He took a black resin, silver inlaid fountain pen from his jacket pocket and began writing in a flowing, neat script. 'I hope I haven't wasted your valuable time, my dear girl. That's the very last thing I'd want. I understand the rigours of your job better than most. But if there's even the slightest chance I saw the car you're interested in that night, you need to know about it.'

Kesey held the door open, the folded sheet of A4 in hand. 'I appreciate your help, sir. If you think of anything else, you know where I am. You can ring or call in person. Either way, I'll be happy to talk to you.'

18

Susan Johnson took a morning shower, shaved her legs, and skilfully applied her make-up, ensuring she looked her very best. Today was the day. The day she'd been waiting for, quite possibly the most important day of her life. Sue felt more excited than nervous. She'd schemed, she'd obtained all the necessary elements of her plan, and Timothy Garvey had it coming. What was there to worry about? Everything was coming together very nicely. All she had to do was stick to her plan and not get caught.

Sue had chosen what she considered a particularly seductive outfit, designed to leave Garvey drooling, a moth to the burning flame. She pulled on sheer black nylon stockings, followed by a matching purple lacy bra and pants set, before slipping into a tight black dress, which she thought of as a perfect final touch, a vision of alluring beauty that no straight man could resist.

Sue looked into the dressing table mirror for one last time, checking the shoulder-length black wig made from real human hair, which framed her heavily made-up face. She reassured herself that the look met her requirements perfectly. Surely even a close friend or relative would struggle to recognise her without looking closely. And the low-cut fringe really couldn't be better. Add the stylish cat's eye glasses with their non-prescription lenses, and a pair of killer heels and the sexy secretary look was complete. She'd be good to go, a tigress ready to pounce, both anonymous and deadly.

Sue checked the contents of her generously proportioned bag for the third time that morning, sorting through the various contents and ticking them off one at a time in her mind. The train tickets, the fast acting sedative drug, the razor-sharp modelling knife and the long, heavy-duty cable ties were all there, together with her ridiculously expensive French perfume, a few dabs of which she now applied to her neck and cleavage, before returning the small bulbous bottle whence it came. Sue picked up a cable tie and tugged it, using all her strength, reassured by its toughness. She'd tested them the day before with the help of Beth, who'd agreed to have her ankles secured before struggling to free herself without any hope of success. Yes, everything was ready. What could possibly go wrong? It was going to be a momentous day.

Sue pulled on her coat, struggling to fasten the three buttons, made more difficult by her long red painted nails, an essential element of her persona. She'd finally decided to leave her coat open, when Ivy knocked on the bedroom door, entering without waiting to be invited. Ivy tapped her watch three times with a concerned look on her face.

'Are you ready?'

Sue nodded. 'Yeah, I think so, I'm good to go.'

Ivy spoke again in hushed, breathy tones. 'Have you got everything?'

Sue's eyes widened. 'I've checked and rechecked.'

'What time's your train?'

'We've got thirty-five minutes. It's not going to be a problem.'

'Are you still okay with Sally looking after the baby? Now's the time to say if you're not.'

Sue's brow furrowed. 'It's a bit late to worry about that now, don't you think?'

'We could still sort an alternative out if you think it's necessary. I don't want you stressing about your little one when you should be focusing on Garvey.'

Sue glanced around as if looking for answers. 'Sally's going to be fine. I've given her all the advice she'll need. It'll be good for her and good for us too. She's starting to trust me. That's got to be a good thing. The Sisterhood may need her someday.'

Ivy nodded. 'I'll check in on her after I've dropped you off. Hopefully, that'll put your mind to rest.'

Sue smiled, her shoulders relaxing. 'Thanks, Ivy, you're a star. I don't know what I'd do without you.'

'It's the least I can do. Us girls have got to stick together.'

Sue picked up her bag, glancing inside to check the contents one more time. 'We'd better get going.'

Ivy took the lead, heading out of the room, across the landing, and down the stairs towards the front door. She checked the street to left and right with quick darting eyes before finally pushing open the security gate and striding across the road to where her four-wheel-drive saloon was parked. 'I've been thinking. It's probably best if I drop you off at Kidwelly Station rather than the one here in town. There are fewer people, it's quieter, you're less likely to be seen.'

'I can't imagine anyone recognising me in this lot.'

Ivy unlocked the car with the click of a button. 'Let's play safe. There's no point in tempting fate.'

Sue climbed into the passenger seat, checking her lipstick in the vanity mirror. 'I'm looking forward to today. It will be good to get it over with.'

Ivy engaged first gear, heading towards the junction leading onto the main road a two-minute drive away. 'Be careful, Sue, the man's dangerous. Remember what he's capable of. There's no room for unnecessary risks. Just do what you've got to do and get out of there as quickly as possible.'

Sue spotted Timothy Garvey standing at the bar in the busy Cardiff backstreet pub within a short time of entering the dimly lit room. He was even bigger than he'd looked in the online photos, taller, and well-muscled in a tight T-shirt that seemed at least a size too small. Sue made a quick visit to the ladies' room before he'd had the chance to spot her, checking her hair and make-up for one final time before heading back to meet him. She thought of the make-up as warpaint, a mask behind which to hide.

'Well, hello, big boy. I thought I recognised you.'

Garvey turned to face her with a broad grin on his very ordinary face. She flinched slightly as he reached in to kiss her cheek, his beer-soaked breath filling her nostrils. 'You're late.'

Sue gave him her best toothy smile. 'I wanted to look my best for you. That takes a bit of time. I want today to be the best day of your life.'

He burped at full volume. 'Drink?'

Sue asked herself if this man she thought no better than a Neanderthal was capable of putting a reasoned sentence together. Maybe the steroids had addled his brain. 'I'll have a glass of red wine, please. French if they've got it.'

Garvey drained his pint. 'Are you staying the night?'

Sue took her coat off slowly, watching his reaction. He was looking her up and down. Lingering where it interested him most. Undressing her with his eyes. 'Oh, I think you know the answer to that. You look as if you can keep going for hours.'

He ordered the drinks, downing half his strong German lager before handing Sue her glass. 'You've made a lot of promises. You've got a lot to live up to. I hope it wasn't all talk. I'm feeling seriously horny.'

She leant forward to gently kiss his lips, hating the touch of him, the smell of his breath. She kissed him again, probing his mouth with her wet tongue for just a fraction of a second before taking a backward step. It left her feeling physically sick. 'Does that give you the answers you were looking for?'

Garvey flexed his powerful shoulders, cricking his neck with a leer. 'I am going to fuck your brains out.'

'Oh, goody, I can't wait. I can be a *very* naughty girl when given a chance.'

'My hotel's only a ten-minute taxi ride.' He squeezed her buttock hard, digging in his fingers. 'Let's get going.'

She felt her gut twist. 'I haven't finished my drink yet.'

He pushed what little was left of his pint aside on the bar. 'I hope you're not a fucking prick teaser.' He cracked his knuckles. 'You'd better not be, for your sake.'

Sue reflected that Garvey was every bit as obnoxious as she'd expected. The slug was repulsive, revolting, or even worse if such things were possible. 'I'm always more relaxed after a drink or two. Be patient, big boy. I'm wet for you. Treat me well, and I'll blow your mind.'

He looked her up and down again, panting slightly, his chest rising and falling in that over-tight shirt. Dark sweat patches were forming under both his arms. 'Five more minutes and we're out of here.'

She reached out, touching his face. 'You've got yourself a deal. You won't be sorry. I promise it will be well worth the wait.'

'You had better not be messing me about.'

She so wanted to slap him. To strike him hard time and again. To dig in her nails, tearing at his face until blood poured from his many wounds. 'I've come all this way just for you. Be patient, let me enjoy my wine, and I'll show you exactly what I came for.'

He scratched his genitals through his jeans, kneading his balls. 'I'm going for a piss. You'd better still be here when I get back. Do not even *think* about doing a runner.'

Sue took a small bottle from her bag as she watched Garvey walk towards the men's room. She turned away, concealing her actions, removed the cap and dropped the entire contents into what was left of his lager, before returning the items to their original location for later disposal. Sue glanced around her as she waited for his return. It appeared no-one was watching. No-one seemed interested. Everything was going as planned. It was easier than she could ever have hoped.

Tim Garvey stood close to the exit a few feet away, beckoning Sue to join him. But she remained seated, crossing one shapely leg over the other so that her short black dress rose up to her thigh. She pointed to his glass. 'You haven't finished your drink yet.'

'I've had enough.'

She got a sinking feeling deep in the pit of her stomach. 'What, a big boy like you? Surely not, I thought you were more of a man than that.'

He walked towards her, picked up his lager and downed it in one. 'I hope you're not going to come up with any more fucking excuses.'

Sue picked up her coat and took his arm. 'Come on, big boy. Let's go find that bed of yours. I'm feeling even hotter than you are. Let's go indulge our fantasies.'

Garvey was already yawning as they left the pub. Sue hailed a passing cab, waving it down a few minutes later. She had to shake him awake when they were seated in the back. He was losing focus, the world around him becoming a confusing blur.

'I don't know what the fuck's wrong with me. I'm feeling like shit all of a sudden.'

'What's the name of your hotel? Tim, *Tim*! Your *hotel*, I need the name of your *hotel*!'

He was slurring his words when he finally provided the answer.

The driver performed an efficient U-turn in the two-lane road, heading back in the direction Sue had come from a short time earlier. 'Is he all right, love?'

'He's just pissed, that's all. The prat's been celebrating a big win on the horses.'

'All right for some.'

'He loses more than he wins.'

Garvey was too woozy to contradict her or even care. He was drooling as he rested his head on her shoulder, a line of spittle running down his chin, wetting her shoulder. Sue attempted to help Garvey from the car on arrival at his modest backstreet hotel, but he seemed close to unconsciousness. His weight was too much for her to manage. Sue bent at the waist, talking to the driver through his open window, allowing her breasts to fall forward, accentuating her already imposing cleavage. 'I really would appreciate your help to get him into the room.'

The driver looked at Sue for a few seconds, then at Garvey still slumped in the back, and then at her again. He had a look of resignation as he exited his cab. 'All right, love. Since you asked so very nicely. He's one lucky sod. How can I refuse?'

'Thank you, that's wonderful. I really appreciate your help.'

The three were met in reception by a middle-aged, brown haired woman who looked from one to another with gradually increasing disapproval. Garvey had been able to stagger in with support, but speech was well beyond him. Sue was the first to speak. 'I am so very sorry about this. I'm afraid my husband has rather overdone things. I think he may have lost his key.'

'There's a five-pound charge.'

Sue took her purse from her bag. 'Yes, of course, I can only apologise for the inconvenience.'

The receptionist handed her a white plastic key card. 'It's room ten down the corridor on your left.'

Sue got a distinct impression that the receptionist hadn't believed a word she'd said. Sue looked at the driver with pleading eyes. 'There's an extra tenner in it for you if you help me get him to bed.'

'I'm in a bit of a rush, love.'

She struggled to prevent Garvey falling, using the wall to support his weight as he slumped to one side. 'How about twenty quid on top of the fare?'

He sighed theatrically. 'We've got him this far together. I may as well help you get him the rest of the way. He's a big lump of a bloke. You're not going to manage it on your own.'

Within a short time, Sue was alone with Garvey, her sat in the room's only armchair, and him stretched out on the bed snoring, naked from the waist down. Sue took off her shoes in the interests of comfort, and spent the next ten minutes or so securing both his wrists and ankles with the strong, heavy-duty ties, ensuring they were all tight enough to prevent any chance of escape if he woke. She was beginning to regret the length of her fingernails, which made each task more difficult than it needed to be. She cursed loudly and crudely on realising she'd forgotten a roll of gaffer tape, but she improvised, stuffing one of Garvey's rolled up socks into his open mouth, ensuring it was behind his teeth to prevent him coughing it out. She entered the bathroom, returning to the bedroom a minute later, where she threw a glass of cold water in his face.

Garvey spluttered awake. He opened one eye and then the other, choking, struggling for breath, unsuccessfully attempting to spit out the sock, and looking up at her with total confusion.

He tried to speak, but no words came, just mumbled, gagging sounds. Garvey appeared more aware of his surroundings now but as weak as a puppy. As large as his muscles were, they were useless.

'Well, welcome back to the land of the living, Mr Garvey. I was beginning to wonder if you'd ever come around at all.'

Garvey bucked first one way and then the other, attempting to free himself with all the strength he had left. But the strong ties held firm, getting tighter with each frenzied movement of his body, cutting through skin and flesh until he bled. Sue watched, mesmerised, a part of her appreciating the spectacle and another part scared that he may somehow free himself.

Garvey continued bucking for another minute or two, his face contorted with a combination of rage and fear until exhaustion finally slowed him almost to stillness. He lay there, still struggling to breathe, his eyes filling with tears.

Sue stripped down to her lacy underwear, removing the wig and glasses for fear of soiling them before they were needed again. Once ready, she took the modelling knife from her handbag. She held it up in plain sight, savouring the panic in his tear-filled eyes, and then ran the sharp blade across her ring finger, allowing a thin trickle of dark blood to drop to the floor. 'Now, look at that. It's as sharp as a razor. That should do the job *very* nicely. Wouldn't you agree, Mr Garvey? Can you guess what's coming next?'

Garvey tried to shout out, but no words came, just more choking sounds as he gagged.

Sue approached the double bed. 'You may be wondering why I'm here, why I'm doing this, why I'm going to tear you apart.'

He shook his head and began bucking again, but to no effect.

'You like hurting women and children, don't you, big boy?

Does it make you feel strong? Does it feed your fragile ego? How powerful are you feeling now?'

He lay still this time, looking at the knife, then at her, and then the knife again. She could see his fear, and smell it too, which did nothing but urge her on.

'I'm reliably informed that you're excited by pain. Not your own, of course, but the pain of others. Innocent people who can't fight back. I'm here to seek retribution. Let's see how you like it. We can take our time. There's no rush. Let's see how many times I can cut you before you bleed to death.'

Garvey lost control of his bladder, flooding the bed with pale yellow liquid as Sue loomed over him, the blade held in plain sight. He tried to pull away as she raised the knife, but she moved quickly, slashing a three-inch gash in his right thigh almost down to the bone. Blood poured from his wound, soaking into the bedclothes.

'How did that feel, big boy? Did you enjoy the experience as much as I did?'

Garvey attempted to roll off the bed to escape her, but she pulled him back with relative ease despite their significant size difference. His eyes looked clearer now, but he was still weak, the drug still in his bloodstream. All his strength had gone. She cut him again, on the other leg this time in the interests of balance, a few inches above the knee. Sue looked from one leg to the other, pleased with the results. She liked the sight of his blood running over his light skin and onto the white quilt. And she enjoyed his distress too, the growing terror and disbelief on his face as if he'd realised his end may be near.

'Struggle, and it will be worse for you, that's no idle threat. Lie still and indulge me, or you'll suffer more than you could ever imagine. I could slice your throat open or cut off your balls.'

The look of horror in Garvey's eyes was changing the contours of his face. If he could have screamed, he would have.

He would have screamed until somebody heard. But instead, he quietly prayed for freedom as Sue raised the knife for the third time. She ran the edge of the blade along the entire length of his muscular body before slashing his right bicep seconds later.

'This is just punishment for all the innocents you've hurt in your sad life. Women like me. Women like my friends and their children too. This is payback. I hope you understand that, Timothy. We convicted you in your absence. It's no more than you deserve.'

She cut his other arm now, and then his chest, before clutching his genitals, digging in her nails as he desperately attempted to twist away. She slashed him and carried on cutting, blood spraying everywhere until he slumped back and still. Finally, she took his penis in hand, slicing it off at the base and throwing it to the carpet with a yelp of delight.

'There, done, you're not going to miss that wee thing for the short time you have left. Maybe you've had enough. Perhaps I should put you out of your misery. Have you had enough, big boy? Are you ready to die?'

Sue stood back to admire the results of her work as the stink of excrement filled the air. 'Oh, dear, now you've gone and soiled yourself. You're not nearly as tough as you thought you were.'

She froze on hearing a sharp rap on the hotel room's door. A female voice Sue recognised as the receptionist's called out, shattering the silence. 'Is everything all right in there, Mrs Garvey?'

Sue closed her eyes for the briefest of moments, replying as calmly as she could. 'Yes, everything's fine, thank you. My husband's been ill, but he's asleep now. Thank you for asking.'

'You know where I am if you need me.'

'I'm fine. Honestly, I'm fine. Sorry for any bother.'

Sue stepped forward, cutting Garvey's throat from ear to ear, before staggering towards the shower, doused in his blood, which ran down her body, dripping onto the carpet, red on grey.

As she entered the small bathroom, Sue was feeling an intense combination of relief and accomplishment, as potent as that experienced at any prior point of her life. The day had ended precisely as she'd hoped. No, no, better than hoped, *much* better, *infinitely* better. Garvey's demise was morally right. She thought it and believed it. His execution was a triumph. A visceral experience bordering on the orgasmic.

But she still bemoaned what she'd become as her high suddenly faded. She winced on seeing herself in the bathroom mirror, dropping to her knees, wishing she could undo the events that had led her on such a path. Maybe if she'd been born into a different family things could have been different. What she wouldn't give to have lived a more ordinary life. A life of love, with people who cared and wished her no harm. But it didn't work out that way, not for her, not even close. And now death was her companion. There was no changing that. Her world was a dark and foreboding place. All she could do was avoid getting caught.

19

Sue left the hotel shortly after dark, creeping through reception unseen and hurrying out into the quiet street just as the rain began to fall. She sheltered in a doorway, pressing herself against a wall, using Garvey's mobile to contact a local cab firm she'd used once before in very different circumstances. 1234, really? Couldn't the muscle-bound fool come up with a more original passcode? It seemed not. The slug was an idiot. A destructive moron who was better off dead.

She waited, wrapped in her coat, buttons unfastened, wig and glasses back on, shivering with cold until a red Vauxhall taxi cab eventually pulled up opposite her about ten minutes later. Sue sat in the back with her collar up and her head down.

'I want you to drop me off at the railway station, rear entrance, and stick to the back streets whenever you can. I don't mind paying a bit over the odds if we can avoid as many cameras as possible.'

Sue looked away when the driver swivelled in his seat to face her. 'You're not in trouble with the law, are you, love? It's more than my licence is worth to help a criminal. They're very strict on that sort of thing.'

She took two crisp twenty-pound notes from her purse and handed them to him with pleading eyes. 'Just leave the meter off, get me to the station no questions asked, and there's another twenty quid in it for you when we get there. That's sixty quid for a ten-minute ride. And then you never see me again. What's not to like? It seems like a good deal to me.'

'Have you been crying, love?'

'Just get me there, please. I'm just about holding it together.'

He started the engine without another word and began driving.

Sue stood in a dark corner of the station platform, looking away as three men wearing Welsh rugby attire slowly approached her. All three were boisterous, loud, and very obviously worse for drink. The tallest of the three, a slim, reasonably good looking young man with short-cropped dark hair, took the lead, stopping immediately in front of her at touching distance. He stank of cigarettes and alcohol.

'Don't I know you?'

Sue recognised two of the three from her home town. Caerystwyth had a relatively small population. If you didn't know someone personally, it was likely you'd seen them around, in the streets, the shops, the pubs and cafés, somewhere. Two of the young men were in that category. The other was a stranger. She turned away, doing her best to ignore the man standing just inches away.

'What the fuck's wrong with you, you stuck-up bitch? I'm only trying to be friendly. You're not all that. Who the fuck do you think you are?'

Sue reached into her bag, clutching the knife, but not showing it. 'I don't know who you think I am, but you're wrong.

I've never seen any of you in my life. I'm standing here trying to mind my own business. I want you to go away and leave me alone.'

He reached out, pulling her coat open. 'Who are you trying to kid? I'd recognise those tits anywhere.'

Sue increased her grip on the knife's handle, picturing herself plunging the blade into his gut and twisting. 'Touch me again, and I'm going to scream for help. My boyfriend's a police officer. You'll be locked up if you're not careful. Sexual assault is a very serious offence.'

'Sexual assault? I only looked at your tits, you stupid bitch. I didn't touch you! You're fucking demented.'

She was about to lash out when another of the three young men pulled her antagonist away. 'Leave her alone, Andy. She's not worth it. She's not who you thought she was.'

The brown-haired young man shouted out as they walked away. 'She's a stuck-up fucking bitch, that's who she is.'

Sue silently swore revenge as the man she now thought of as Mr Brown walked away with his companions one drunken step at a time. Her mind was racing, faster and faster, one thought after another tumbling in her mind. She'd find out who he was, develop an online relationship, meet him, and then sink in her claws. Just as she had with Garvey. And just when Mr B least expected it. She pictured herself slashing his throat right down to the bone, and felt a little better almost immediately as a surge of adrenalin flooded her bloodstream. A part of her wanted to follow him now. To get him alone. To rip him to pieces. But she somehow resisted the temptation despite its almost over-whelming allure. Now was not the time. The risks were too high. Getting caught was never a part of her plan.

Sue watched as the three men staggered onto the train she'd initially intended to catch before this change of plan. Mr B made an obscene gesture to her as he boarded, and she knew in that instant that she was going to make him suffer more than any man had ever suffered before. Yes, her childhood abuser had escaped prosecution. He'd avoided just punishment for the abominations he'd inflicted on her at such a young age, the invasive touching, the robbing of her childhood innocence.

But this one would pay. Yes, he'd pay the ultimate price, when he'd finally screamed his way to silence. He'd be begging to die before the end. Desperate for the grave before she finished with him. She'd cut out his tongue. Poke his eyes out. Slice his ears off. And his dick too. See how he liked that. He wouldn't be so mouthy then. His time would come.

Sue sat in the waiting room, tears rolling down her face, glad of the limited warmth a lukewarm radiator offered as the outside temperature continued to drop close to freezing. She was using her own phone now, having discarded Garvey's mobile in a nearby bin. Sue scrolled through various social media and dating sites in search of her prey.

She started with pages relating to Caerystwyth, the rugby clubs, and then young Welsh men named Andy, finding Mr B surprisingly quickly even for her. The bastard was a college student, studying agriculture, no less. A slug who should know better. A rat who should understand the damage he caused with his touching and ranting disrespect. That made it worse in her eyes, much worse, the ultimate crime. Mr B really did deserve to come to a horrible end. And soon, he would. She'd make sure of that.

Sue spent the next half hour waiting for the next scheduled Caerystwyth train, and mentally rehearsing the worst forms of human torture in her mind's eye. The more pain she conceived, the more sadistic her thoughts, the happier and more stimulated she felt inside. It was a self-therapy of sorts. Or, at least, that's what she told herself. The hunted became the hunter. Killing those who preyed on the innocent was a means of feeling better.

And the fact that her clandestine activities protected other inno-cents was an undoubted bonus, a service to society that should be appreciated and applauded. Predatory men had to be punished. That seemed obvious. It went without saying. Someone had to do it. Someone had to stop them. So why not her?

20

Lewis was sitting alone in the police headquarters canteen, picking at his meal less than enthusiastically, when Kesey joined him at the table. She sipped her hot coffee and grinned.

'Roast chicken and a green salad. I never thought I'd see the day. I'll mark it on the calendar for posterity. Hang on, where's my phone? I'll take a photo. They may want to report it in the force magazine. Raymond Lewis is on a diet. That is worthy of note.'

Lewis chewed a chunk of dry, unseasoned chicken and swallowed, forcing it down his throat. 'I don't want to talk about it. You can take the piss as much as you like. I'm going to ignore everything you say.'

Kesey tried not to laugh. 'No, it's all good, Ray. I'm pleased for you. You could do with losing a bit of weight. So no more chocolates for you. I'll eat them all myself from now on. I'm there for you every step of the way.'

'If you haven't got anything useful to say you can sod off and leave me alone. Things are bad enough without your contribution.'

She adopted a pensive expression. 'On a serious note. What did you make of the captain's evidence?'

'Oh, so we're back to work now, are we?'

'I'd be interested to know your thoughts.'

'He claims he saw a red Fiesta which may or may not have been the one owned by Beth. He saw a driver who may or may not have been a bloke. It doesn't help us at all. I wouldn't even call it evidence. It's next to useless. Does that sum it up well enough for you?'

'Have we got anything else?'

'We had the usual nutters ringing in wanting to confess to all sorts. But that was it.'

Kesey took another sip of coffee, her expression serious. 'Tim Garvey was killed.'

Lewis perked up immediately. 'I was hoping for a bit of good news. Another scrote bites the dust. Tell me more. When, where, and how?'

'A maid found him cut to pieces in a Cardiff hotel earlier today. I've had a DI from the South Wales force on the phone, a John Wilson. He isn't someone I've come across before. Do you know him?'

Lewis shook his head. 'No, he must be new. I can't say I do.'

'Garvey was found in one hell of a state, apparently. Someone had tortured him before finally cutting his throat right down to the bone. The room was plastered in blood, the bed, the floor, the walls, everywhere, even the shower. Wilson described it as a slaughterhouse. The worst crime scene he'd ever seen. The maid had to be sedated. Hardly surprising, if you think about it. It must have been one hell of a shock.'

Lewis pushed his plate aside, most of his meal uneaten, the salad untouched. 'Have South Wales got any idea who killed the scrote?'

'Garvey arrived at the hotel in the company of an adult

female and a male taxi driver at about 2pm yesterday afternoon. The male left very soon afterwards. He was there for maybe five minutes at most before driving off. Garvey seemed either drunk or drugged. He was uncommunicative, staggering. The male helped get him to his room. The woman introduced herself as Garvey's wife. She hasn't been seen since. South Wales have ruled out the driver as a suspect, but the woman is a definite person of interest.'

'Kim Garvey? Really? She's not the violent type. That seems highly unlikely to me.'

Kesey shook her head. 'No, there's no way it was Kim. The woman didn't match Kim's description, not even close. Wrong height, wrong build and hair colour. And anyway, I've checked, Kim's been laid up ill at her boyfriend's flat. It's all on Facebook. I spoke to him. He's been keeping a close eye on her. There's no way Kim went to Cardiff. She's got that flu that's doing the rounds. Just getting around the flat is difficult enough for her. I confirmed that with her GP. She hasn't left Caerystwyth. I've told South Wales that's a virtual certainty.'

'Garvey's upset a lot of people over the years. He's got a lot of enemies.'

'It looks as if he finally pissed off the wrong woman. There must be any number who'd be glad to see him dead.'

'But not many who'd actually do it. The killing you described was frenzied, the product of psychotic rage. Any woman who's capable of doing that is likely to do it again.'

'I've been thinking the same thing. And if it was a woman, it's rare. It's more usually a man's crime. Wouldn't you agree?'

Lewis slurped his tea, which wasn't nearly as sweet as he liked it, two sugars instead of three. 'It's another coincidence.'

'Look, I know what you're going to say. I wasn't expecting any different. Another death linked to the refuge. Blah, de, blah! But Garvey died in Cardiff, well off our patch. He likely met his killer there. Maybe he was unlucky. He hit on the wrong woman, someone with serious mental health problems who happened to have a knife handy. Harper was hit by a car and Garvey was sliced to pieces. The MOs couldn't be more different. It's a different killer, that's blatantly obvious. If there's a link to the refuge, it's tenuous at best. Kim isn't even living there anymore. It just happens that both victims were abusers with a long history of violence. It's a coincidence, just that, a coincidence, nothing more. You're seeing links where they don't exist.'

Lewis appeared far from persuaded. 'What did she look like, this woman at the hotel? Have we got a description?'

Kesey rolled her eyes. 'Oh, here we go. We've got to leave it to the South Wales force. It's not our case. And anyway, the woman may have had nothing to do with the murder. She may have been abducted. She could be dead herself. You need to let it go.'

'Just tell me what she looks like.'

Kesey held her hands up above her head as if surrendering at gunpoint. 'Okay, okay, she was in her thirties, Caucasian, of average height and curvy. Happy now? You're like a dog with a bone.'

'She didn't happen to have shoulder-length blonde hair, did she?'

'Where's that coming from?'

'It may be worth checking out where Susan Johnson was at the relevant time. It's a long shot. But it's got to be worth a try. She knows Kim well enough. She knows Harper's ex. She's certainly curvy. We know very little of her background. Maybe she's done both women a favour.'

'Oh, come on, Ray, you get fixated far too easily. And it's not helpful. The Cardiff woman had jet-black hair, not blonde, black with a long fringe. Have you got that? And she wore plastic-framed glasses. It wasn't Sue Johnson. The description isn't even close.'

Lewis massaged his belly, which was rumbling loudly enough to be heard. 'I may have a quick word with Ivy anyway. Maybe Sue's dyed her hair. It's worth asking. And anyone can wear a pair of glasses. Maybe she didn't want to be recognised.'

'You do *not* want another complaint. Not after the last time. I had to talk Halliday out of suspending you. Harassing domestic violence survivors isn't going to do you any favours at all.'

Lewis made a face. 'Ivy's an old mate. She won't mind having a chat. And I'll be subtle about it. What harm could it do?'

Kesey thought that *subtle* wasn't a word she'd ever use to describe her sergeant. Abrasive maybe, loud, determined, stubborn, yes, but subtle, no. 'Knock yourself out, Ray. I know you're going to talk to her whatever I say. But don't waste too much time on this. Talk to Ivy, put your mind to rest and then move on. We're looking for Harper's killer. Garvey isn't our problem. You're looking in the wrong direction. I don't want to have this conversation again.'

21

Lewis hugged Ivy, pulling her close and kissing her cheek before following her into the comfortable, well-furnished sitting room of her quaint, detached Caerystwyth cottage on the leafy outskirts of town. Lewis noted that the room smelt of cats and furniture polish, neither of which he found offensive. He happily accepted the offer of coffee and a slice of homemade sponge as he sat himself down on the three-seater floral patterned sofa, sinking into the cushion. His diet wasn't going well. Lewis liked his sugar. He silently conceded that eating was one of the few pleasures he had left.

Ivy disappeared into the kitchen, reappearing a few minutes later carrying a silver tray laden with a delicious looking two-layered Victoria sponge, white porcelain plates, and a stylish Portmeirion coffeepot, milk jug and sugar bowl set, gold on black. She placed the tray down on a low 1970s teak-veneered table and sat down opposite her visitor with a beaming smile on her friendly face. 'Shall I be mother?'

Lewis nodded, looking first at her and then the sweet treat on offer. He could quite easily have eaten the entire cake. But a slice or two would have to do. 'It's good to see you again, Ivy. It's been a while. I was sorry we didn't have time to chat at the refuge the other day. I'm pleased to make up for it now. It's been too long.'

'How's Emily doing? She was what, maybe nineteen or twenty the last time I saw her?'

'Yeah, she's fine, she's still in Manchester. She met her husband at university and never came back.'

'It happens sometimes.'

'So I hear.'

'Give her my best when you next speak to her.'

'I will.'

Ivy handed Lewis an overly generous portion of sponge filled with a layer of jam and whipped cream, followed by his coffee, to which he added three sugar lumps initially, followed by a fourth after tasting.

'What can I do for you, Raymond? As nice as it is to see you, I know this isn't a social call.'

He glanced to his right as a black cat with diamond-bright yellow eyes jumped through a half-closed window, settling on the mat in front of the gas fire. 'Am I really that transparent?'

She laughed. 'You most certainly are. You always were, and you always will be. You were always after something. I'm sure today's not any different.'

Lewis picked up his slice of cake. He spoke as he ate, revelling in the sweet airy texture. He attempted to sound as casual as possible when he said, 'I don't know if you've heard, but Tim Garvey's been killed.'

She fumbled with a knife. 'Garvey?'

Lewis thought it an unexpected response. 'Yeah, you must know of him, Kim's husband. She hasn't long left the refuge.'

She pulled her head back. 'Ah, yes, of course, Tim Garvey. When did this happen?'

He took another bite, relishing the combination of cream and jam. 'He was murdered yesterday afternoon.'

'Did it happen locally?'

There was a look of surprise on the detective's face. It wasn't an obvious question. 'He was killed in Cardiff. Why do you ask?'

Ivy cut Lewis a second slice of sponge. Even bigger this time. Her hand was trembling slightly as she passed it to him. 'I appreciate you letting me know. But I don't usually get a personal notification, even when one of my girls is involved. What's this really about, Ray? Kim is no longer my responsibility. What's all this got to do with me?'

He nibbled at his cake while weighing up her responses in his analytical mind. It seemed suspicions came with the job. 'I'm... er... I'm a bit confused, to be honest, Ivy. Laura Kesey mentioned that she'd already had a word with you about Garvey. I don't understand why anything I've told you came as a surprise.'

Ivy fidgeted with her cuff as the cat sauntered across the floor, jumping up and settling on the arm of her chair with an easy grace. 'Laura enquired after Kim, but she made no mention of her husband. Does Kim even know he's dead? She has a right to be told, surely.'

'I'll call and have a word with her once we're done here if that makes you feel any better.'

'I'll give her a ring to warn her you're coming.'

'I'd prefer if you didn't.'

Ivy stroked the cat, which had now climbed onto her lap, purring. 'Why would you say that?'

Lewis struggled to find an adequate answer. Something that wouldn't put her on her guard. 'It's a procedural thing. It's something I need to do myself.'

'Please be gentle with her. It's going to come as a shock. Kim was scared of the man but she wouldn't want him dead. It's not in her nature. And she hasn't been at all well recently. Please bear that in mind. She's very easily upset.'

Lewis considered leaving it there. Maybe he should go without asking any more. Kesey would undoubtedly think so. He imagined her Brummie tones speaking to that end. But his dogged inquisitiveness soon overcame his reticence as he knew it inevitably would. 'This is going to seem like a strange question but I'm going to ask it anyway. Are you aware of Susan Johnson's whereabouts yesterday afternoon?'

Ivy was quick to answer, snapping out her reply. 'She was at the refuge all day. Why do you ask?'

'Has she not got a job?'

'She works part-time in a local care home. She's planning to train as a social worker.'

Lewis ate the last of his sponge before rising to his feet. He was about to say his goodbyes when he decided to ask one last question. 'What colour is Sue's hair these days?'

Ivy looked up at him and frowned. 'You always were a strange one. What on earth are you asking me that for?'

'Just answer the question, please, Ivy. Believe me when I tell you I need to know.'

'It's blonde, it's always been blonde. She's single if that's where this is going. I heard that the two of you got on rather well when you visited. I could sound out if she's interested and let you know if you like. Although she's a lot younger than you are. You must realise that. Maybe you should aim a little lower.'

Lewis blushed crimson. 'Have you ever seen her with black hair and or glasses?'

Ivy laughed. 'Not a chance, her hair's always been one shade of blonde or another, ever since I've known her. She often jokes that blondes have more fun. And she wears contacts, never glasses, not even for reading. She's a very image-conscious lady.'

'Okay, thanks, that's helpful.' He paused, and then added.

'You wouldn't ever lie to the police for one of your girls, would you?'

She led him towards the door. 'We have known each other for a very long time, Raymond. I'm going to say this only once and I want you to listen. Whatever you're thinking, you're wrong. Sue is one of the nicest people I've ever had the privilege to meet. She wouldn't harm a fly. And as for suggesting I'd lie, I'm not angry, I'm disappointed. You should know by now that you can trust my honesty and judgement. Your job has changed you, and not for the better. I'm beginning to wonder if I ever really knew you at all.'

22

Michael Pearson sat waiting in Swansea Prison's visitors' hall, watching the seconds tick by on the wall clock until Jonathan Goodman finally turned up ten minutes later than expected. Pearson had been wondering if Goodman would arrive at all. And his relief was almost overwhelming when he first saw Goodman's face at the entrance. But Pearson hid it well. The ability to mask his feelings mattered to Pearson. It was a skill he believed could help keep him safe in a dangerous world.

Goodman, a sharply dressed accountant in a well-fitted, three-piece charcoal-grey business suit, had a bad-tempered and sulky look on his face when he walked across the room to join Pearson at a small table secured to the floor. Goodman spoke in hushed tones, keen not to be overheard by a nearby guard or anybody else who happened to be listening. 'Was threatening me really necessary? What the hell have I ever done to you?'

Pearson snarled his reply. 'It was one phone call. What's the big deal? I had to get you here somehow. You wouldn't have come otherwise.'

Goodman sucked in the air. The situation felt like a bad dream that was all too real. 'What's this about? I'm not in the habit of visiting prisons. I want out of here as quickly as possible.'

'You should have thought about that before buying illegal drugs, Jonathan. What was it, now? Let me think. A few ounces of cocaine and a bit of pot. Oh, and there was that one time you wanted to try heroin. The best hit of your life. That's what you told me. You sent me texts, never a wise move where illicit drugs are concerned. If you thought we were friends, you were *very* sadly mistaken. I took screenshots every single time you contacted me, an insurance policy if you like. You never know when these things could come in useful. And now, here we are. You are going to do *exactly* what I tell you to do, or your respectable big-time career is well and truly over. A trusted friend of mine will put printed copies of everything you wrote in the post addressed to the drug squad.'

Goodman was desperate to be somewhere else entirely, anywhere but there. He was experiencing a growing sense of alarm, unsure of what to do or say for the best. 'But if you report me it leads straight back to *you*. You'd be in as much trouble as I'd be, more, if anything. You're a dealer. We'd both be prosecuted.'

Pearson leant back in his seat and laughed. 'That's almost certainly true, but then, you've got a lot more to lose than I have. I'm a criminal. I'm used to this shit. But you'd be different. Prison destroys people like you. Do you really want to take that risk? You'd be eaten alive.'

Goodman unfastened the top button of his shirt, his hands moving in short, twitchy movements. He closed his eyes for a beat to calm his breathing. 'What do you want from me? Is it money? Is that what you're after? Why not say if it is? Drop the bullshit!'

'Well, a few quid's always welcome. It's not such a bad idea. I may well take you up on that kind offer one of these days. But for now, I've got something else in mind, something much more important.'

Goodman looked away and then returned his gaze to the source of his irritation. 'Just tell me what you're after and let me get out of here.'

'You seem in rather a rush, Jonathan. What's your hurry? Don't you like me anymore?'

Goodman formed his hands into tight fists below the table. 'Get to the fucking point, or I'm on my way.'

'Oh, naughty, naughty, that's not the attitude I'm looking for. What's that good-looking young wife of yours going to do if her drug-addled husband is banged up with no cash to pay the bills? I'm guessing she'll be shacked up with some other hairy-arsed bloke before you can turn around. Someone else is going to be tapping that tight little pussy.'

Goodman's body suddenly sagged, his earlier show of boldness a mere memory. 'I'll beg if you want me to. Or you can tell me what the fuck you want. I've worked hard to get where I am. And I want to stay there. I'll help you if I can.'

Pearson gave a short slow clap. 'Very well said, now that was much better. You may avoid prison, after all. I've had plenty of time to think while I'm here. One of the few advantages of incarceration. I need an alibi. A solid defence that would stand up in court. From someone without a criminal record, someone like you. It's your new purpose in life.'

Goodman's mouth fell open as a clammy hand flew to his chest. 'Are you saying you expect me to lie to the police?'

'Ten out of ten, you've got it. I think "attempting to pervert the course of justice" is the correct legal term. But stay calm, stick to the story I'm about to outline, keep repeating it if asked, and you should be fine if you don't shit yourself and screw things up. I'll be out of here, happy as a sandboy, and you can carry on screwing that hot little tart of yours to your heart's content. It's a win-win all around. It's either that or the offending texts are forwarded to the boys and girls in blue. Which is it going be? Make your choice.'

Goodman spread his fingers wide on the table in the shape of a fan, as if supporting his upper body for fear of falling forward. Pearson thought it a dead giveaway. Goodman's body language told him all he needed to know. The man was crumbling under the pressure.

'Come on, Jonathan, look me in the eye, there's a good lad. I asked you a question. The clock's ticking and I require an answer.'

'If I do this, that's the end of it, yes? Do you guarantee there'll be no more demands?'

Pearson grinned. The meeting was going better than he could ever have hoped. He'd expected more resistance, even a point-blank refusal, or maybe counter threats to challenge his own. Goodman was a big bloke. He looked as if he should be able to handle himself. Who knew he'd be such a pushover. And he'd fallen for the bluff so very easily. Without even asking to see evidence of the texts. It was almost too good to be true. 'Do this one thing for me, and I won't ever bother you again, that's a promise. And you can have as much cocaine as you want, my treat. Just the once, mind, don't get greedy.'

'What do you need me to say?'

'Okay, listen carefully: this matters. I'm in here for giving my girlfriend a few miserable slaps. No more than she deserved. Sally's an obnoxious bitch at the best of times. I need you to tell the pigs that you saw me at the time of the assault. I was shopping in town just as I claimed during the interview. You're absolutely certain of the time and date. You'd swear to that in any court in the land. I can't possibly have been beating the crap out of Sally at the time she claimed. She was either lying or mistaken. That's going to be more than enough to scupper the case if you stick to your story. Even if the pigs think you're lying, they can't possibly prove it.'

The look of disgust on Goodman's face betrayed his revulsion. 'You're here for beating up a woman? Why would you do that?'

'What the fuck does it matter what I'm here for? It doesn't change anything.' Pearson glanced at the wall clock. 'We've got ten minutes before you're kicked out of here. This is your last chance to agree before I get on the blower to grass you up. Make your choice. My contact's waiting for my call. Are you going to help me or not? Yes, or no, which is it going to be?'

'It makes no sense. How could I possibly know the details of the case?'

'You say the friend of a friend works at Caerystwyth Police Station. They shot their mouth off after a few drinks. You can't recall the name.'

Goodman held his head in his hands, covering his face. 'This is crazy. It's far too complicated.'

Pearson smiled coldly. 'I'm going to go over the details, and you're going to remember them. Do I make myself clear?'

Goodman's face was ashen as he looked back at the prisoner. 'All right, I'll do it. Tell me everything I need to hear. But it's a one-off. Once this is done, I don't ever want to hear from you again.'

23

Kesey shook Goodman's hand before inviting him to sit. She'd already realised that her interviewee was nervous. That was blatantly obvious, unmistakable. But she didn't yet know why. She planned to find out at the earliest opportunity.

Kesey reached across the table to shake the accountant's hand, noting it felt clammy despite the outside chill. She looked into his eyes and got a distinct impression that he was trying to appear a great deal more relaxed than he felt. She quickly decided that a formal approach was best. There was tension in the air. The man was crapping himself. He claimed to be there as a witness. But something was undoubtedly amiss. She was desperate to find out what.

'My name is Detective Inspector Laura Kesey. I'm told you're here to discuss the Michael Pearson case. Is that correct?'

Goodman shuffled uneasily in his seat. 'Um, yes, that's right, it's something that's been bothering me since I saw a report in the local paper. I can't get it off my mind. I'm a concerned citizen. I'm here to do the right thing.'

Kesey found herself doubting every word he said. Nothing about Goodman rang true. She pushed a single sheet of an A4 paper across the table, a tactic she'd used before. It gave her a chance to think. 'Let's start with your name, address and full contact details. I like to know who I'm talking to.'

He patted his pockets. 'Have you got a pen?'

She handed him a clear plastic biro and watched as he began writing. His hand was trembling. He seemed to have trouble gripping the pen. It was either nerves or illness. She strongly suspected the first rather than the latter was the more likely explanation. She studied what he'd written, raising it closer to her eyes rather than use her reading glasses, which were on her office desk. 'Is there something worrying you, Mr Goodman? I can get you a glass of water if that would help? You seem a little shaky.'

She thought she saw him flinch.

'I'm sorry, it's... er... it's just that I'm not used to this sort of thing. I've never been in a police station before. I don't know where to start.'

Kesey continued staring at him, refusing to look away. The interview was already feeling strangely unlike any that she'd experienced with other potential witnesses. More akin to an interview under caution, with a suspect. 'How about you start at the beginning? I usually find that's best.'

'Okay, I'm just going to say it.'

'You do that, Mr Goodman, talk away, I'm listening. I may take a few notes while you're speaking. It's useful to have a record of your precise words. If we need to check your claims, you understand. I need to be sure that everything you tell me is accurate.'

He was red in the face now despite a half-open window letting in the winter air. When he spoke, he blurted out the words. As if he couldn't get them from his mouth fast enough. They sounded strangely convoluted. As if he'd prepared them in advance. 'I have excellent reason to believe that Mr Pearson didn't assault his girlfriend as she claimed.'

Kesey made a quickly scribbled note in her pocketbook before raising her eyes. 'Which girlfriend are you referring to? You need to make it clear. There's no room for ambiguity. This is too important for that.'

'I think her name's Sally. Has he got another one?'

The detective stiffened. 'I'll ask the questions.'

'I'm sorry, I didn't mean any offence.'

'Do you know Michael Pearson? You're both local. You're of similar age. Is he a friend?'

He shook his head. 'I knew *of* him, but I wouldn't say I *knew* him, no. And we're certainly not friends. That's not why I'm here, if that's what you're thinking.'

She made another written note, taking her time. There was something about Goodman that Kesey didn't like. She didn't like him at all. 'That seems a bit complicated. Why didn't you just say you don't know him and leave it at that?'

'I'm sorry if I'm not expressing myself clearly enough for your liking. I'm not finding this easy. I don't know the man.'

Kesey drummed the table with the first three fingers of her left hand. 'So, if we make enquiries, acquaintances, social media, emails, phone records, that kind of thing, we won't find any links between the two of you. Is that what you're claiming?'

Goodman looked ready to run for the door. 'I should probably mention that I've lost my phone.'

'That's convenient.'

'Actually, it's anything but. I'm here because it's my civic duty. If I can help avoid a miscarriage of justice, surely I should. I can't understand your attitude. I thought you'd be happy to see me.'

'Are there any links between you and Pearson, or not? It's a simple enough question that requires an answer. Just a yes or no will suffice. It won't be hard to confirm one way or the other.'

'I did... er... I did visit him the one time in prison.'

'Ah, okay, *now* we're getting somewhere. Why would you visit the man if the two of you are strangers? You need to explain yourself. And this had better be good. I'd remind you that I'm taking notes for the official record.'

'I... er... I needed to tell him that I knew he was innocent. I couldn't have lived with myself if I'd left him there to rot. I've got a strong social conscience. It felt like the right thing to do.'

Kesey rested her elbows on the table. 'And how would *you* know he's innocent? I suggest you think very carefully before you answer. I interviewed the victim. I saw her injuries. The girl was black and blue. Making a false statement is a serious criminal offence carrying a potential prison sentence.'

'Everything I'm saying is the truth. I'd swear to that in any court in the land.'

Kesey poised her pen above her pocketbook. 'Oh, you would, would you? Let's hear it then. I'm interested in finding out what you've got to say for yourself.'

Goodman spent the next few minutes recounting his version of events as Kesey listened in silence with increasing suspicion and concern. The more he said the less she liked it. His words seemed rehearsed. As if he'd practised them in advance.

'Is that it? Are you finished?'

'Yes, that's it. I've said everything I came here to say.'

'And you can't for the life of you remember the name of the person you talked to. The person who just happened to know the full details of Pearson's case. And you can't even describe them to me.'

He gave her a sideways glance. 'I'm sorry, no.'

'That seems *highly* unlikely to me.'

'I saw Pearson in town at the time I said I saw him. I'm certain of that. I've got no doubt in my mind. Isn't that what matters? He can't have been beating his girlfriend and shopping in town at the same time.'

'And are you ready to confirm all that in a formal written statement? You're running out of opportunities to withdraw your claims.'

He stalled for a second before responding. 'Yes, I'm ready. That's why I'm here. Let's get on with it.'

'Pearson beat that girl so very badly that she had to be hospitalised. She was in one hell of a state. Her nose was fractured, she lost a tooth. Do you understand the possible legal implications of what you're about to put in writing, both for you and for her?'

'Everything I've told you is true. I don't know how many times I have to repeat myself.'

Kesey stared at him without speaking for a full five seconds, a cold expression on her face. 'What's he got on you, Mr Goodman? I know there's something.'

'I've told you the truth, nothing but the truth.'

She took a statement form from the drawer. 'Have it your way. I've given you every opportunity to change your mind. Let's make a start. A written statement it is.'

24

Lewis stood in his boss's office doorway, resting his bulk against the frame and said, 'Put a smile on your face. It may never happen.'

Kesey's skin bunched around her eyes in an aggrieved expression he'd seen before in times of disappointment or crisis. She wore her heart on her sleeve. 'It's bad news.'

Lewis entered the room. 'Oh, God, it's not the family, is it?'

She shook her head slowly. 'The CPS has dropped the Pearson case. He's going to be released.'

Lewis stepped forward. He drew his leg back and kicked Kesey's metal wastepaper bin hard, bouncing it off the nearest wall with a resounding clang before it fell back to the floor. 'Oh, for fuck's sake, that's *crazy*! That accountant who came in was lying through his teeth. Why drop the case? I've never heard anything so *ridiculous* in my life.'

There was audible stress in Kesey's voice when she responded. 'I agree with you, Ray. I couldn't agree more. But we couldn't prove it. He made a full written statement. He stuck to his story. And he's got no history of dishonesty. Or at least nothing the CPS could use against him. On paper, Goodman's a model citizen. From the defence point of view, that makes him a good witness.'

Lewis slumped into the nearest chair, his chest getting tighter with every passing moment. 'What about the fact that the scrote visited his scumbag friend in prison. The bastards are in it together. That one visit says everything to me.'

'I know what you're saying. I think the same way. But the CPS has made their decision. It's a done deal.'

'Don't they need the leave of the court to discontinue?'

'Not if they consider it in the interests of justice.'

He held his hands wide, palms forwards, fingers spread. 'Talk to the bloke in charge. Tell him they've made a mistake. Persuade him to change his mind.'

Kesey slammed the side of a clenched fist down on her desk. 'Do you think I haven't tried? Had Sally been willing to appear as a prosecution witness, it would have been different. But she wasn't. Goodman's statement was the last straw. It contradicts Sally's allegations in the worst possible way.'

Lewis wasn't ready to let it go. 'What about Halliday? Couldn't he do something?'

She lowered her gaze, speaking more quietly now. 'It's too late for that, Ray. The decision's made, the case has been dropped. Everyone concerned has been notified, and Pearson gets released. There is *nothing* anyone can do, not me, not you and not Halliday. We've got to suck it up and accept it however badly it stinks.'

'You said *everyone* has been told. Does that include Sally?'

Kesey sighed. 'No, it doesn't, not yet, that's down to me. The girl's already disillusioned with the system and now this. She's never going to trust us again. And who could blame her? Certainly not me.'

'I am going to fucking well nail Goodman for something the first chance I get. I'll beat the truth out of the bastard if I have to.'

Kesey pointed at Lewis with a jabbing finger, her voice rising in volume and pitch. 'You don't go anywhere near him, Ray. You know what you're like when you're angry. You'd go too far. There's nothing to be gained. Stay away! And that's an order in case you were wondering.'

He avoided her eyes. 'When are you planning to talk to Sally?'

'As soon as we're finished here. Pearson will be out this afternoon. I can't delay talking to her for very much longer. I'm going to do it in person rather than over the phone. I owe her that much.'

'Do you want me to let Ivy know you're coming?'

'No, you're all right, thanks, mate. That's something I need to do myself. Do you fancy a quick coffee before I go?'

'Yeah, go on then, why not? And a few biscuits if they're on offer.'

'I thought you were on a diet.'

Lewis laughed, his big gut wobbling like a birthday jelly. 'Yeah, so did I. Maybe next week.'

Kesey swivelled in her seat. She leant to her side and switched on the kettle, suddenly lost in her own thoughts. It hadn't been a great day, and things would soon get worse. Such were the burdens of small-town policing. Could life get any better? Yes, it flaming well could.

25

Kesey reached out, touching Sally's arm. 'I am so very sorry. I know it's bad news. I wish I could tell you something different.'

Sally covered her face with her hands and began weeping, quietly at first, but then with greater intensity, her angst pouring from her in a torrent as she sank to the floor.

Kesey sat at her side. She was glad that Sally had suggested they speak in her room as opposed to one of the communal rooms. At least the poor girl had some privacy to mourn. Thank God for small mercies.

'Is the b-bastard coming back t-to Caerystwyth?'

Kesey placed a gentle hand on the young woman's shoulder. 'There's no easy way of telling you this, but Pearson's innocent in the eyes of the law. He can go anywhere he wants. He'll likely be back in town later today.'

Sally curled up in a tight ball, her back curved, her head bowed, and her limbs bent and drawn up to her torso. She was emitting a series of low, feeble sounds now, which gradually evolved into a long, mournful cry that echoed around the room.

'You're safe here, Sally. I've spoken to Ivy on your behalf. Your room's yours for as long as you need it.'

Sally stopped weeping as quickly as she'd started. She uncurled, rising to a seated position on the carpet, dark mascara smudged across one cheek. 'Why did you get my hopes up? You're full of crap! You all are. Every single one of you people. I shouldn't have listened to a word you said. Sue said you'd let me down.'

What to say? What on earth to say? Kesey tried to find a response. Anything that would ease Sally's concerns even slightly. 'We'll be keeping a close eye on Pearson. There's a panic button in the hallway. If he as much as threatens you, he'll be rearrested.'

'What, like last time you mean?'

'All the police can do is work within the law.'

'Mike beats the crap out of me, then he's arrested, maybe he spends a bit of time in prison, or maybe he doesn't. But either way, he's soon back out on the streets again, and I'm back in the shit. Maybe I'll have a bit of luck, and someone will run the bastard over like they did Louise's ex. I'll keep my fucking fingers crossed.'

For the first time, Kesey asked herself if Lewis could be correct. She still thought it unlikely. But assumptions were dangerous in police work. It was worth checking out. 'Is Harper's death something you talk about here at the refuge?'

'Sue says he had it coming.'

Kesey softened her tone. 'Ah, all right, that's interesting. Does she know who did it?'

Sally stood now, her hands resting on her hips. 'Of course she frigging well doesn't. Why would she? You want to get out there and arrest some real criminals, not bother the likes of us.'

'I didn't mean to imply anything.'

'I should frigging well hope not.'

'How's Kim coping after her husband's death?'

Sally approached her bedroom door, holding it wide open. 'What the fuck's going on here? You come here to tell me you've fucked up any chance of Mike serving time. And now you're asking questions about my friends. You should be ashamed of yourself.'

Ivy suddenly appeared in the doorway, a look of concern on her face. 'I couldn't help but overhear the heated voices. Is everything okay in here?'

Sally spoke up before Kesey had the chance to answer. 'DI Kesey was just about to fuck off and leave me alone.'

Ivy exhaled, more a groan than a breath. 'Come on now, Sally, I know you're upset, but you know what I think about bad language. Please think of the children.'

'I'm sorry, but this cow has wound me right up.'

Ivy turned to Kesey, who'd already decided it was time to leave. 'News of Pearson's release was rather a disappointment, Laura. Is there nothing you can do?'

'I'm sorry, as I've already explained to Sally, it's a done deal. If there was anything I could have done to change the situation, I would have done it. I'm not any happier about his release than you are.'

Ivy strode into the room, stopping only inches from the detective, looking directly into her eyes. Kesey could feel her breath on her face. 'Why is it always the women who suffer? The law seems to do so little to protect us. Surely you'd have to acknowledge that you've let Sally down.'

'Sally, if you hear from Pearson, let me know immediately. And please talk to a lawyer. I've told you that before. There *are* legal protections that can be put in place. There's more than enough evidence for an injunction.'

Ivy took Sally's hand in hers, squeezing it tightly before speaking again. 'I think it's time for you to leave, Laura. You've let Sally down, you've let me down, and worst of all you've let yourself down. I'm more disappointed than angry. If my girls can't rely on a senior female officer, who can they rely on?'

Kesey stepped out onto the landing with Ivy close behind. 'I did what I could. Everything that happened was beyond my control.'

'It's always someone else's fault. That sounds strangely familiar.'

Kesey bit her tongue hard as she hurried down the stairs. She'd never felt more regretful or frustrated. 'I'll see myself out, ladies. Don't hesitate to contact me if you need me. I can't promise you'll get the result you want. But I can guarantee I'll do my very best for you. No-one can do any more than that.'

26

Kesey shook her head on meeting her sergeant's tired eyes. 'Do you know, you've actually had me asking myself if the women at the refuge know more about the recent killings than they're letting on. I still don't think it's likely. And I certainly don't think any of them are directly involved. But someone may have heard something. There was something about what Sally said to me today that got me thinking.'

Lewis slurped his beer, savouring the yeasty froth at the top. 'Well, praise the Lord, you've actually seen the light. About time.'

'I wouldn't go quite that far. It was a passing thought, no more than that. There's a lot of rumours going about town, all of them crap. The refuge girls probably have their own theories. That's all I'm thinking.'

Lewis took another mouthful of beer. 'Yeah, but you're not as sure as you were. You're starting to doubt yourself. You can tell your Uncle Raymond. I'm not going to bite.'

Kesey smiled, amused as intended but still a little irritated. She sipped her lager shandy. 'I still think it's highly likely we're talking about two very different murderers. Harper's killer is very probably local, operating within a zone of comfort, as Grav used to say. I'm willing to bet they knew Harper would be out running that night, and they knew where he ran, too. Either they'd been watching him, or they knew him well. That could be any number of people. But starting with his close contacts makes absolute sense. We've looked at most of them. And, as for Garvey, his killer may not be from our patch at all. And I don't think she was. He likely picked her up in Cardiff, either there or online. South Wales tell me he had a reputation for being into kinky sex. He met a lot of women, most of them for one-off dates. Very few ever saw him twice.'

'I had that chat with Ivy. She's adamant that Sue Johnson was with her at the relevant time.'

'Oh, here we go again. You need to let it go, Ray. How many times do I need to say it? The descriptions don't match, you've already told me Ivy can be trusted, and Sue hasn't been convicted of a traffic offence, let alone anything relevant. It's entirely inappropriate to think of her as a suspect. Leave it to South Wales. It's their case, not ours.'

Lewis drained his glass, licking his lips as the last of the malty liquid ran down his throat. 'Do you want another one of those?'

'No, you're all right, thanks, mate. I promised Jan I wouldn't be late.'

'Do you mind if I have one?'

'You don't usually ask. Who am I, your mother?'

He approached the bar, returning a short time later with a third pint in hand. 'Anything new on Pearson?'

'He was released this afternoon.'

'There's no fucking justice.'

Kesey pushed her glass aside, still three-quarters full. 'Sometimes there is, and sometimes there isn't, that's the truth of it. We can't win them all.'

'We should have won that one.'

She nodded. 'Yeah, we should have.'

'How did it go at the refuge?'

'Don't even ask.'

'That bad?'

'Worse!'

He moved forward in his seat. 'I've been doing a bit of house-to-house in Ferryside. One of the locals thinks he saw a red Fiesta in the village a few days before Harper's killing.'

'Why haven't you mentioned it before?'

Lewis shrugged. 'It may be something and nothing. They didn't see the number plate. They couldn't remember the driver. It may not even be the same car. Beth's car wasn't the only red Fiesta in Wales. They're a popular model.'

She stood, preparing to leave. 'It's a potential lead. We need to follow it up.'

'I'll pop down there again in the morning and knock on a few doors. I was planning to anyway.'

'Take two of the DCs with you. You'll get it done more quickly that way. And let me know if you hear anything interesting, no surprises. I want to be kept in the loop. I've got an update meeting with Halliday tomorrow afternoon. It would be nice to have something positive to tell him.'

Lewis laughed, head back, mercury fillings in full view. 'I'd rather you than me. You don't want to come to Ferryside with me instead, do you? We could have an ice cream on the beach.'

Kesey waved as she walked away, speaking without looking back. 'I only wish I could, Ray. I only wish I could.'

27

Halliday left Kesey sitting waiting in silence for over five minutes while he continued reading a sheaf of papers behind his unnecessarily large desk. Kesey believed she knew exactly what he was doing. Making her wait again, trying to make her feel unimportant, signalling his own seniority as was his custom. No surprises there, he did it almost every time they met. And it was as infuriating this time as it had been on every other occasion. More exasperating, if anything, his methods were becoming old and tired. Kesey crossed and uncrossed her legs, brushing a tiny fleck of white cotton from her purple trousers. She contemplated how much time she'd wasted in recent months while a man she thought ridiculous boosted his brittle self-worth in one way or another. She noticed that her breathing was a little louder than it had been.

'Are you going to be much longer, sir? There are things I need to get on with.'

He looked up, peering over the top of his reading glasses. 'Did you say something, inspector?'

Kesey was sure he knew exactly what she'd said. 'I'd be

grateful if we could get on, sir. I'm due at the local social services office at four o'clock.'

He laid down his paperwork with a dramatic sigh. 'What the hell are you doing going to social services of all places? You should be concentrating on your priority cases. I would have thought that was obvious even to you.'

Kesey tapped a foot against the floor, fidgeting. 'That's precisely what I'm doing.'

He snapped out his reply. 'Perhaps you could expand on that for me.'

'Evidence obtained by DS Lewis earlier today suggests that the car used to run down and kill Harper was seen in Ferryside, the estuary village where he lived, three days before the murder. A local man has made a statement to the effect that he saw the driver, who matches the description of the owner, an Elizabeth Williams, known as Beth. As you know, she reported the car stolen after the event. The village isn't somewhere you pass through without intent. It's not en route to anywhere else.'

'That's all very well, Laura. But what's it got to do with social services? You really need to express yourself more clearly.'

A vein pulsed in her neck. 'We know little of Beth's background. I've arranged to meet with the local adult services team manager. She's agreed to allow me to read the relevant file. There may be something in Beth's history that's informative.'

'Even if the driver seen by this local man was Elizabeth Williams, it may mean nothing at all.'

'I'm well aware of that, sir. But it's something we need to pursue. If it was Beth Williams, we need to establish what she was doing there. Ray often says he doesn't like coincidences. And this is starting to seem too much of a coincidence to me.'

Halliday flashed a cold smile. 'Aren't I correct in thinking that Williams has an alibi for the time of the killing?'

Kesey silently swore as her blood pressure increased. Her

head began to ache. The patronising bastard was asking questions he already knew the answer to. 'Yes, sir, Beth provided an alibi which was checked out and confirmed by DS Lewis.'

'I seem to recall that the Johnson woman you refer to stated that Williams was somewhere else entirely at the relevant time. That is the very definition of an alibi. I hope you're not wasting your time. And, more importantly, wasting mine.'

'Susan Johnson wouldn't be the first witness to lie. We need to pursue the matter further. That's all I'm saying. Given the new information, we can't accept the women's version of events on face value. You'd be the first person to criticise my failings if we did.'

He shook his head with a sneer. 'Tread carefully, Laura. You're on very thin ice. It would not look good if we're thought to be harassing a group of domestic violence survivors. The chief constable would be less than impressed. The press would have a field day.'

Kersey glanced at her watch, asking herself why time seemed to be passing so very slowly. 'I'm planning to ask DS Lewis to interview Beth one more time once I've had an opportunity to peruse the social services file. Should I go ahead or cancel? I'd prefer you to tell me now rather than complain about it afterwards.'

He visibly stiffened. 'Is Lewis capable of subtlety?'

She nodded twice. 'Ray's a good detective.'

'Then I suggest you go ahead with caution. But supervise the process very closely. I'm not nearly as confident in Lewis as you seem to be. And watch your tone, Laura. I don't appreciate your attitude. Please remember who you're speaking to. I'm getting a little tired of your lack of respect.'

She noted that her jaw felt so very tense. She was used to Halliday's excesses. Why let it get to her so very badly? 'Do you want an update on the Pearson case while I'm here, sir? I've still got five minutes.'

'You've got as long as I tell you you've got, Laura. Social services can wait.'

'Shall I take that as a yes?'

'Just get on with it. You can drop the attitude. I'm seriously questioning if you're up to the job.'

Kesey massaged the back of her neck as her headache intensified. 'Pearson was released from prison following the discontinuance. One of our uniformed constables saw him this afternoon. He's definitely back in town. His young victim has been notified of the situation and advised to apply for an injunction. We will, of course, support the application. I understand that social services are facilitating an application for compensation. The girl suffered some serious physical and psychological injuries. Pearson poses a significant danger both to her and to any other woman with whom he develops a relationship.'

'The case hasn't exactly covered you in glory, has it, Laura?'

Her headache began to pound. 'The events leading to Pearson's release were totally beyond my control. I still think the CPS's decision to discontinue was both premature and ill-advised, but it was their decision, not mine.'

'Yes, so you claim.'

What the hell was that supposed to mean? 'I'm simply telling you what happened.'

He looked down at Kesey for what felt like an age before speaking again. As uncomfortable as it became, she refused to look away.

'How long have you been a DI, Laura?'

She stood, preparing to leave. 'I was promoted shortly after DI Gravel left the force. Why do you ask?'

'I think this may be the time to ask a more experienced officer to take over the Harper case. You seem a little out of your depth. If you're not coping, you need to tell me. I'm sure I could find some less demanding duties for you to perform. Something more suited to your skill set.'

'I'm coping just fine.'

'Yes, so you claim, but I'm not nearly so sure. Close the door on your way out. You've got forty-eight hours to make some significant progress. Fail to do so, and I'm going to have to seriously reconsider your future role. Sometimes officers are promoted beyond their ability. I strongly suspect that you're one of those.'

28

'You haven't got an aspirin, have you, Ray? Halliday is winding me right up.'

Lewis delved into one pocket after another, his jacket first followed by his trousers. 'What's he done now?'

'All his usual shit. I don't know what's wrong with the bloke. I'd like to kick him right in the balls.'

Lewis passed Kesey a half-used strip of aspirin, some of which he always kept handy. 'Wouldn't we all? Perhaps we should form an orderly queue.'

She grinned. 'Fancy a coffee?'

'Yeah, why not?'

'We're out of biscuits. I meant to pick some up when I was out, but it slipped my mind.'

His disappointment was written all over his face. 'Canteen?'

'I'm a bit pushed for time.'

He handed her a mug filled almost to the brim, slurping his own. 'Any joy with the social?'

Kesey popped two tablets into her mouth, chewed, and swallowed. 'Beth had a very ordinary life before she met the man who changed everything. You must remember the Smith case. Harry Smith, another bastard who was released far too soon.'

'Didn't Sharron deal with it?'

'Yeah, that's right, before she went off on maternity leave.'

'Where's Smith now?'

'He's still local. He hasn't reoffended since he's been out. Or, at least, not that we know about. He did allege he was being stalked by someone unknown a few weeks back. Tanya took a statement, but no-one took it seriously.'

Lewis chuckled to himself. 'What a tosser! After everything he's done. You'd think he'd want to stay well clear of the law.'

'The manipulative git treated Beth well while he was grooming her. But it all changed very quickly once they moved in together. It was all the usual shit. Alienating her from friends and family, threats, criticisms, controlling everything she said and did, and using his fists when it suited him, but never where it showed. Over time he completely destroyed her confidence and self-esteem. She moved into the refuge on his release.'

'Same old story.'

Kesey sipped her coffee. 'I've got every sympathy for the woman, but that doesn't mean she shouldn't be re-interviewed. Let's see if she confirms she was in Ferryside that day, and if she does, why.'

'Do you want me to do it?'

'Yeah, I think that's best. But interview her at the refuge this time rather than her workplace. You can get her on her own and take as long as you need.'

'Do you want me to re-interview Sue while I'm there?'

Kesey shook her head. 'No, or at least, not yet, not unless Beth changes her story. Sue's made her statement, and I still think it's likely the two of them were telling the truth. I just want to be sure. Let's take it one step at a time.'

JOHN NICHOLL

He drained his mug. 'Okay, message received. I'll sort something out tomorrow.'

'Thanks, Ray, it's appreciated as always.'

He scratched his chin. 'I still think I should pay Goodman a visit. To mark his card if nothing else. I couldn't believe how quickly the CPS dropped the case. If they'd given us a bit more time, things could have been different.'

Kesey had a *here we go again* look about her. 'I want you to forget about Goodman and concentrate on the Harper case. Don't lose focus, Ray. Halliday put me under a lot of pressure. We need to make some progress. Maybe he'll follow through on one of his threats for once.'

'I wish he'd fuck off back to the Met.'

'I'd throw a party. It would be better than winning the lottery. Nothing could please me more.'

29

Sally peered through a narrow gap in her bedroom curtains, almost entirely hidden as she looked down on the street below. Pearson had been out there for over half an hour, not doing anything to draw undue attention to himself, merely standing there in the evening shadows staring up at the refuge building, his eyes moving from one window to the next, from right to left, up, down, and back again. Sally called out to Sue, who was sitting on the single bed behind her, cradling her child.

'He's still there. What the hell's he doing? He's just standing there with an angry look on his stupid face. What's that about? I really wish he'd go away.'

'He's trying to scare you, Sally. I've told you. Come away from the window. If he sees you, he'll think he's winning. It'll only encourage him. Ignore the bastard for long enough, and he'll lose interest.'

'What if I phone the police?'

'Don't waste your time. The scheming bastard isn't breaking any laws. He knows exactly what he's doing.'

Sally peeped out again, dropping to her knees. 'Oh, shit, he's crossing the road towards the gate! What if he gets in? What if he gets in, Sue? The man's a psycho! What are we going to do?'

'Right, come away, hold the baby.'

Sally was whimpering as she crossed the room on all fours. She was fighting to control her fear as she climbed onto the bed, a thin dribble of urine soaking into her jeans around the crotch. 'Come on, little one.' She rested the small child over one shoulder, gently patting his back. 'The nasty man will be gone soon. Yes, he will. Yes, he will.'

Sue threw the curtains aside, opening the window wide. She placed her head out, glaring down at Pearson, who was making urgent efforts to climb the gate, so far without success, as the soles of his shoes slipped on the smooth metal. Sue shouted out, her shrill tone echoing in the street below. 'I know exactly who you are, you pathetic excuse for a man. Sally's not here. She's moved on. I suggest you fuck off before the police arrive. There's nothing here for you. They're already on their way.'

Pearson looked up at her, spittle spraying from his mouth as he yelled a stream of angry abuse. 'Oh, I know she's in there, bitch. I can smell her. Shut your lying mouth or I'll shut it for you.'

Sue closed the window tight, followed by the curtains, leaving just a slight gap through which she could peep. 'Put the baby down, Sally. Put him in his cot and call Ivy. My phone's not charged. It's down to you. Now would be a good time to dial 999.'

'I think Ivy's already g-gone home.'

Sue watched as Pearson pushed a sizeable green plastic wheelie bin up against the gate, and then he climbed onto it, clambering over the top of the gate and dropping to the ground within a few short feet of the front door. Sue turned to Sally, who appeared frozen in indecision. 'Ring, just *ring*! Come on, now, Sally, do it, the bastard is trying to get into the building. I don't want him in here with the baby in the house. Dial 999!'

Sally handed the baby to Beth, who had appeared at the bedroom door. Sally patted her pockets, spotting her mobile on the carpet next to the bed. She dropped to the floor, grabbing it with frantic fingers. 'All right, all right, I'm doing it, I'm doing it.'

Sally held the phone to her face. She requested the police, providing all the information requested by the call handler.

'Be quick, the bastard's hammering the door. I think he's–he's trying to break it down.'

Sally looked on with a mix of fearful disbelief and admiration as Sue took a knife from her bag and began descending the stairs two steps at a time. Sally watched from the landing as Sue hit the red button alarm on the wall to her left, and then began yelling while pounding the front door almost as violently as Pearson, who had taken a backward step. Sue continued shouting, screaming above the wailing of her baby. She became louder and more agitated with every second that passed. 'Fuck off, you inadequate twat! How dare you come here. You piece of shit! You sad excuse for a man.' She held the knife high above her head behind the door's reinforced glass panel and continued ranting. 'Come in here, and I'll tear you to pieces. Let's see how tough you are then, you slimeball. I'll slice your fucking face off!'

Pearson attempted to shake the security gate open as a siren sounded in the distance, getting gradually louder. Sue became suddenly calmer as a patrol car pulled up outside the refuge. She threw the knife up the stairs onto the landing. 'Pick it up, Sally. That's it, pick it up. Put it back in my bag, and then hide the bag under your bed for safekeeping. Do you understand?'

Sally confirmed that she understood as she retreated back to her bedroom, still distressed but calmer than she'd been. She noticed that her jeans were wet for the first time. She watched from the window as two uniformed constables escorted their cuffed prisoner towards a waiting police car. Sue was still shouting, less noisily now, but still more than loud enough to be heard. 'That's it, drag the stupid bastard away. He's scum, a slug, the lowest of the low. Maybe you can actually make the charges stick this time. It's about time you did!'

Sue suddenly stopped yelling as abruptly as she'd begun, panting and then laughing until tears ran down her face, smudging her make-up, as she began climbing the stairs.

Sally hugged her friend, thanking her from the bottom of her heart. Sally was still a little shaken, but Sue's heightened emotional reaction was infectious. Sally laughed too, not as heartily as Sue, but laughter nonetheless. It was more a release of tension than anything else. Sally so wanted to be like her friend as they stood there on the landing. Sue's reaction to Pearson's invasion of their territory was a side of her Sally had never seen before. But it was a side she decided she liked – a side she admired. For the first time, Sally understood Sue's words and applauded them. *You're a tiger. Sink in your claws. The world should hear you roar.*

30

J an met Kesey's eyes and smiled. 'How about a romcom?'

'Yeah, why not? Have you got any particular one in mind? I could do with cheering up.'

'I noticed that Jack Nicholson comedy we like on the movie channel. You know, the one with Helen Hunt as his love interest.'

'*As Good As It Gets*?'

'That's the one. I know we've seen it loads of times, but it always makes us laugh.'

Kesey nodded. 'Sounds good to me.'

'There's a big bag of popcorn in the cupboard if you fancy it? We could imagine we're at the cinema snuggling up in the back row like we used to.'

Kesey made her way to the kitchen with a laugh. 'I'll bring two bowls.'

'And some wine. There's half a bottle of white in the fridge that needs finishing.'

Jan was searching for the TV remote when the house phone rang out in the hallway. She cursed quietly and coarsely as she went to pick it up. 'Hello, Ray. I thought it was probably you.

Laura's on her way, I can hear her coming from the kitchen. Yeah, I'm good thanks, and Ed too. How about you?'

She listened to the response.

'Laura mentioned that you've been on a diet... Oh, hang on, here she is. I'll just pass her the phone.'

Jan glared at Kesey as she passed her on her way back to the lounge. Sometimes a look could suffice. What was the need for words?

'Hi, Ray, we were just about to watch a film. What's up?'

Kesey pressed the phone to her ear as her sergeant outlined the earlier events at the Curzon Street refuge.

'So, is Pearson still in the cells?'

Lewis confirmed that he was.

'And he claims Sue threatened him with a knife?'

Lewis replied in the affirmative, followed by his take on events.

'Okay, so even if Pearson is telling the truth, Sue was behind a closed door with him ranting and raving on the other side, making all sorts of threats of violence. The women know his history. They know he's dangerous. Even if she did grab a knife, it sounds a lot like a panicked attempt at self-defence to me. And that's if it's anything at all. I'd say charge Pearson and leave it at that. I don't see the need to consider any action against Susan Johnson. I can't see it serving any useful purpose.'

Kesey glanced towards the lounge as Lewis clarified her earlier orders.

'Yeah, that's right, carry on and re-interview Beth as planned. And have a quick advisory word with Sue too. Make it clear that brandishing a weapon is rarely a good thing even in the most extreme of cases. If Pearson had managed to break into the building, he could well have grabbed it and used it against her... Oh, and I'm planning to have a word with Sally myself. Leave that to me. The poor girl must have been terrified. She already thinks I let her down. I want to make it clear I'm still there for her. It's the least I can do in the circumstances.'

Kesey frowned hard as Lewis made his final comments.

'No, Ray, I don't think we need to notify South Wales Police about the incident with the knife. Why would we? I wouldn't even call it an incident. And you seem to be forgetting that Susan Johnson has a solid alibi for the time of Garvey's murder. And as if that wasn't enough, she bears no resemblance whatsoever to the woman seen with him shortly before his death. I don't know what goes on in that head of yours sometimes. I'm telling you she's not a suspect. She never was. It's time to let it drop.'

31

The overcast dappled-grey sky was threatening snow by the time Lewis pulled up his car about twenty yards past the Curzon Street refuge early the next morning. He hurried towards the entrance, suddenly aware of the winter chill, pressing the bell – now repaired – three times and waiting until Susan Johnson opened the door followed by the high-security gate, which squeaked for the need of oil. Sue was smartly dressed, in full make-up, smiling warmly, and holding her baby with care and affection. She stepped aside, allowing Lewis to enter the pleasantly warm, primrose-yellow hallway. 'You're an early bird this morning.'

'I've arranged to have a chat with Beth before she heads to work, but I'd like a quick word with you too if you've got time.'

He thought he saw the hint of concern on her face before it became another smile.

'Let's use the kitchen. I'll put the kettle on. Tea or coffee?'

Lewis sat at the pine table, his heavy legs spread wide. 'Coffee, please, love, milk and three sugars.'

He was a little taken aback when she handed him the baby, but he didn't object. He just held the child, a little awkwardly at first, but then with growing confidence as memories of his own early parenting came to mind. It wasn't precisely the interview scenario he'd intended, but it would have to do.

Sue looked back on approaching the fridge. 'I've got some nice single cream here if you fancy it?'

'You're spoiling me.'

'I'm here to please.'

'We need to talk about what happened when Pearson turned up.'

She placed both coffees on the kitchen table, then picked up her child from his arms. 'I thought that's what this was probably about.'

'Pearson mentioned that you had a knife.'

'Oh, God, no, I've always been such a good girl. I'd hate to be in trouble with the police.'

Lewis slurped his coffee, leaving a creamy residue above his top lip. He wanted to put an arm around her. To comfort her. But he resisted. 'Look, I know you were scared, that's entirely understandable. Tell me what happened.'

'Okay, right... er... Sally was sobbing upstairs, looking after the baby. Ivy had already left. And I was absolutely terrified. Pearson had climbed over the gate. He was hammering on the front door trying to break it down, and I panicked. I totally freaked. I went completely to pieces. I'd never been so scared. I was in fear for my life. I ran into the kitchen and grabbed a knife. I know I shouldn't have, but I did.' She laughed humourlessly. 'I don't know what I thought I was going to do with it. I'd have wet myself if he'd managed to get in. I can't believe I did it now. It was so unlike me. I'm usually such a wimp.'

At that moment, as Sue looked deep into his eyes, Lewis felt inclined to believe her, his prior suspicions alleviated by her reasoned response and demure demeanour. 'You don't need to worry about it, love. I've had a word with DI Kesey, and we've both decided that you were acting in self-defence. You know of Pearson's history, you know he's dangerous to women. So what you did was entirely understandable. There won't be any further police action. You acted instinctively in the heat of the moment. No-one can blame you for that. But, with that said, I don't ever want you to do anything like that again. Do you hear me? If he'd got in, you could have ended up being stabbed yourself. So, no more knives. Are we agreed?'

Sue dropped her eyes and nodded. 'I don't know what I was thinking. Thank you so very much, sergeant, you've been truly wonderful. Such a kind man. You've got no idea how much I appreciate your help.'

Lewis drained his cup. 'Right, I think we're done here. If you could call Beth for me, that would be helpful.'

Sue stood, still cradling the baby. 'I'm sure she already knows you're here. Nothing stays secret for very long in this place. I'll tell her we're finished. Oh, there is one thing.'

'What's that, love?'

'I hope you don't mind me asking. Would you be willing to give me your contact details in case I ever need you? It would make me feel so much safer if you could. It would mean a lot.'

He delved into one jacket pocket and then a second, finally fishing out a badly creased card stained with blue ink. He offered it to her with an outstretched hand. 'There you go, love, no problem at all. That's my office number and my mobile. Give me a ring anytime. I'll be pleased to hear from you. And don't worry about what happened with Pearson. It's forgotten. Put it out of your mind.'

She beamed, stepped forward and pecked his cheek, leaving a faint lipstick imprint on his sallow skin. 'Thank you so much, Ray, I really appreciate all you've done. I wish all men were like you.'

He looked back, blushing. 'It's all part of the service.'

'I'll just get Beth.' And with that, she left the room.

Beth entered the kitchen a minute later. Lewis thought she looked a little sheepish as she closed the door behind her. Yes, she looked nervous, as if fearing what the interview may bring. It didn't necessarily mean anything, but it could.

'Sit yourself down, Beth, there's things we need to discuss.'

She followed instructions, choosing a chair at the end of the table, as far away from him as possible. 'I thought I'd answered all your questions at the café.'

'Something's come up.'

Beth's shoulders curled over her chest. 'I've already made a statement. I thought this was over with. Do I need a solicitor?'

'We're having an informal chat for now. If that changes, we'll continue at the police station.'

She looked close to tears. 'What do you want to ask me?'

'Have you ever been to Ferryside?'

She answered immediately, without even a second's delay. 'Yes, I have, a couple of times. It's a nice place. I'd passed through on the train and liked the look of it, especially the beach. It's got a great view of the castle across the water.'

Lewis had been half-expecting a denial. He asked himself if her original statement were true despite his earlier doubts. 'When was the last time you were there?'

'Um, it was – It must have been a few days before that poor man was run over and killed.'

'Can you remember the exact day?'

'I'd say it must have been the Tuesday because I had an early finish. I left work after the lunchtime rush was over. It was a quiet day, and the manager decided we were overstaffed.'

'So, what took you to Ferryside?'

'It was a pleasant sunny day, cold but nice and bright. I fancied some time to myself. And I thought, why not enjoy a walk on the beach? It's usually so quiet: I like that.'

Lewis thought her story rang true. If she were guilty, why say she'd been to the village at all? But he still had some doubts. Nagging doubts that wouldn't let up. 'Did you travel by car or by train?'

'I drove. It's only eight miles from town, twenty, maybe twenty-five minutes at most.'

He turned the page of his pocketbook, holding his pen above the paper, preparing to record her next reply. 'Were you aware that Harper, the murdered man, lived on the outskirts of the village?'

He thought he saw a tension in her face. As if she was carefully considering her response. 'No, I had no idea. Why would I? I didn't know the man. I wouldn't have recognised him even if I'd seen him.'

He stood, pushing himself up with the arms of his chair. 'Okay, thank you, Beth, that's it for today.'

'Will I have to make another statement?'

'No, I don't think that's necessary for now. I've made a note of what you've told me. That should suffice.'

She looked up at him with pleading eyes. 'I want you to catch that man's killer as much as you do. You do realise that, don't you, sergeant? I think it may be the only way you'll leave me alone.'

'I'll be on my way. Thanks for your co-operation. Give my best to Ivy.'

There was a loud knock on an upstairs window as Lewis hurried across the road in the direction of his car. He turned and looked up to see Sue waving at him. She had a glowing smile on her beautiful face as she blew him a kiss.

32

Sue sat in Ivy's typically middle-class sitting room sipping peppermint tea from a china cup decorated with multi-coloured roses. Ivy cut her a generous slice of rich fruit cake before getting down to business.

'Tell me how things went with the fat detective.'

Sue nibbled at her cake, picking out a particularly juicy sultana with her front teeth before responding. 'I think he was on a fishing exercise more than anything else. I don't think he really knows very much at all. He was probing for information, nothing more than that. But I did get a distinct impression that he's still suspicious, that's the bottom line. I was praying Beth wouldn't say anything stupid if he put a bit of pressure on. She's close to folding under the stress. If he sees her again, if he keeps on at her, she may let something slip. I think that's our biggest worry.'

'I've been thinking. Maybe it would be worth you getting to know Raymond a little better. Why not get close to him? Get him to trust you. Let's find out exactly what the police know. And you could point him in the wrong direction. It shouldn't be difficult, not for you. You've told me he likes you. You'd have him chomping at the bit in no time. Use your feminine wiles to your full advantage. He wouldn't stand a chance.'

'Are you considering getting rid of him?'

Ivy sipped her tea before placing her cup back on its matching saucer. 'No– no, I don't think so, or, at least, not as yet. I've known Raymond since we were children. I was a friend of his sister. And I'm still rather fond of him in a strange way. Like a flea-ridden pet dog you've got used to over the years, or a comfortable pair of slippers you can't bring yourself to throw out. He always was a meddling busybody sticking his big red nose in where it didn't belong. I wasn't in the least bit surprised when he joined the police force all those years ago. He likes snooping into other people's business, but he's not an evil man. If we do end up having to kill him, then so be it. These things have to be done. But I'd want it to be a last resort, and as painless as possible, for his sister's sake as much as his. I'd want to be sure we'd done all we could to negate any risk he poses by other means before resorting to execution, however well justified. I don't think that's unreasonable.'

Sue opened and closed her mouth before finally speaking. 'What's one man's life compared to the work of The Sisterhood?'

'You haven't taken on board what I've said, Sue. All I'm saying is let's keep our options open. Raymond may well be more useful to us alive than dead. Flatter him, massage his ego, and he'll be eating out of the palm of your hand in no time. Who knows what he'd tell you. The information you glean could be invaluable. You'll be our listening ear in the viper's den.'

Sue's lips pressed together in a slight grimace. 'As long as we're not ruling out killing him all together. We can't let sentimentality get in the way of our mission. It's far too important for that.'

Ivy's expression darkened. 'That isn't what's happening here.

I've told you what I think. I've made my decision clear. I'm perfectly capable of reaching rational conclusions whoever's involved. We can re-evaluate if the situation changes. Let's leave it at that.'

Sue looked away. 'I could give Lewis a ring, ask him out.'

'You do that, let's see where it takes us.'

'He gave me his mobile number. I'll contact him tonight.'

'How's Sally doing after that unpleasant business with Pearson?'

Sue pushed her cake around her plate. 'She's putting on a brave face, but the girl's crapping herself. You should have seen him, the man's a total psycho. She's not going to relax until she's free of him.'

'Maybe it's time we did something about it.'

Sue nodded. 'I've been thinking the same thing. What have you got in mind?'

'Let's get Sally officially initiated into our Sisterhood first. And then we'll deal with Pearson. We need to be sure she's suited to our group. It's not for everyone.'

'I've got to know her pretty well. I'm certain she'll be up for it.'

'I'm sure you're right.'

'When are you planning to meet?'

'I'll need to talk to the others,' said Ivy. 'Everyone needs to be there. There's no point in going ahead otherwise. I was thinking here on Monday evening at the usual time. How does that suit you?'

'I'll need to check if Louise's eldest can babysit, but that should be perfect for me.'

Ivy smiled. 'In that case, I'll pencil it in the diary. All power to The Sisterhood!'

Sue punched the air. 'All power!'

'Are you going to stay the night?'

'I was hoping you'd look after my little one. There's somewhere I need to be.'

'At this late hour? Is it anything I need to know about?'

'Not really, just an itch I need to scratch.'

Ivy looked across at the baby, happily sucking on a dummy in his pushchair close to the hearth. 'Of course I'll look after him. It'll be a pleasure. It will be lovely to have the company. It's usually just the cat and me.'

Sue rose to her feet. 'Thank you, Ivy, you're the best. I'd better make a move. It's getting late. I need to be on my way.'

33

Sue broke into Andy's rented residential caravan a short time before he arrived home from a nearby pub. She prised open a window and hid in a wardrobe to the side of his bed, waiting with increasing impatience until he finally climbed under the covers almost an hour later. Sue's muscles were stiff and threatening to spasm as she imagined the end game. But the endorphins released by her reaction to the bloody images in her mind helped alleviate her pain.

She peeped through a small gap in the wardrobe's double doors, watching as Andy, or Mr B as she still thought of him, switched on a silver coloured laptop that appeared past its best. He positioned himself on the bed in a seated position, his body supported by a large pile of pillows. Sue couldn't see the computer's screen, but the loud, unconvincing female yelps and groans of feigned delight told her all she needed to know. Andy's hand began to move up and down under the covers, getting gradually faster, followed a minute or two later by a far more convincing groan of his own. He wiped himself with the black T-shirt he'd been wearing earlier, threw the soiled garment aside, placed his computer on the caravan floor next to the bed, and lay down flat for the first time that night.

Within ten minutes, Mr B's eyes were closed, and Sue could hear the intermittent sound of soft snoring as his chest slowly rose and fell under the winter-weight quilt.

Sue pushed open the doors in the semi-darkness, creeping towards him as he rolled over, snorting, and then settling, talking nonsense in his sleep. She held her knife tightly in her right hand as she approached his side, moving slowly with caution until close enough to press the razor-edged blade firmly against his windpipe. She looked down at his youthful face as he opened his eyes, somewhere between troubled sleep and wakefulness. Sue increased the pressure of the blade against his exposed skin, drawing a few drops of dark blood, which looked black for the lack of light.

'Well, hello there, Andy. This isn't a dream. And that's a knife in your throat, in case you weren't sure. Move, and you'll be dead in seconds. Remember me?'

His eyes narrowed as he shook his head ever so slightly.

'Don't tell me you've forgotten me already. Cardiff Railway Station, me, you, and those two drunken mates of yours. I'm the "bitch" you shouted abuse at. You wanted to look at my tits. Do you remember me now? Nod your head very, very slowly if you do.'

A look of horrified recognition dawned on the student's face as he raised his head and nodded just a fraction of an inch.

'There you go, you do remember me. Top marks, what a clever boy you are. And you should be clever too, what with you being a college student and all. But not clever enough to avoid a psycho bitch like me. I'm a tiger, Andrew. You picked the wrong woman to abuse. I'm here to sink in my claws.'

He suddenly spun his athletic body, turning towards her, attempting to grab her knife-hand. But Sue moved with surprising pace, jumping back with the grace and agility of a dancer, avoiding his reach as he lurched towards her for a second time. Sue drew back her arm, bringing her knife hand forward with speed and power, sinking the blade deep into his abdomen right up to the shaft. She was crying silent tears as she stood there nose to nose with her victim as he slumped forward, twisting the blade first one way and then the other.

'Does that hurt, Andrew? You screamed loud enough. It seems to be hurting to me.'

He staggered backwards and then fell to his knees. 'Call an ambulance, please. Please help me. I'm losing... I'm losing a lot of blood.'

'Oh, I don't think so, Andrew. You sealed your fate that day in Cardiff. Did you enjoy upsetting me? Did it make you feel big? Do you like humiliating women? Is that what turns you on? It seems that way to me.'

He clutched his wound, attempting to stem the blood flow with applied pressure, but to little effect. 'Help me, please, I'm begging you. I was pissed. I'm sorry! Call me an ambulance. Please! I don't want to die.'

Sue crossed her arms, hugging herself as his voice began to fade. She didn't hear him anymore, just a voice in her head reminding her of her troubled childhood. Sue walked towards him one slow step at a time as he fell first to all fours, elbows resting against the caravan's floor, and then on his side with his knees curled up to his chest. He was still trying to talk, but his words were barely audible, just whispers only he could comprehend.

'I knew a man like you as a child. I killed him once I was old enough to do it. And I got away with it too. My tormentor made me the woman I am today. Aren't you the lucky one? That's why I'm here. Sometimes I think it would have been better if I hadn't been born at all.'

Sue raised the knife high above her head and stared down at him, her mind drifting back in time, his face morphing into that of her childhood abuser as if he were back to taunt her all over again. Tears filled her eyes as she choked on her words, forcing them from her mouth. 'You're g-guilty of the worst possible crime, as guilty as sin. I sentence you to d-death as your judge, jury and executioner. Pray for your soul. It's time to meet your maker.'

34

Lewis knocked on Kesey's office door before entering, unusual for him. She was just finishing a call when he sat himself down.

'Coffee?'

Lewis shook his head. 'Nah, I haven't long had breakfast.'

Kesey studied him closely. 'What's up with you? What have I missed? Why have you got that stupid grin on your face?'

He looked back sheepishly. 'I've got a date on Friday night.'

She bit the inside of her cheek hard, trying not to laugh. 'I never thought I'd see the day. Who's the unlucky lady?'

'Oh, yeah, very funny, hilarious as always.'

'No, who is it, is it someone I know?'

All of a sudden Lewis didn't seem quite so full of himself. 'It is, as it happens.'

'Come on, I want a name.'

He raised a hand to his chin. 'Right, if I tell you, I don't want you going on about it. Have we got a deal?'

'Deal!'

'It's Susan Johnson, the woman from the refuge.'

Kesey's head tipped to one side. 'You what? Sue? Are you winding me up?'

'She's not a suspect. You've told me that often enough. Why shouldn't I take her out for a bit of food and a drink?'

'How many reasons do you want?'

Lewis approached the window, facing away from her, looking out at the distant green countryside beyond the car park. 'The woman rang and asked me out. She asked me, not the other way round. And I've agreed to it now. It's a one-time event. I can't change my mind. How would she feel if I rejected her? She's been through enough shit. I don't want to let her down.'

'I seriously wonder about your judgement sometimes. You've done some really crazy things since I've known you. But this beats them all.'

About ten seconds passed before he spoke again. 'Did you hear about that kid who died in the caravan fire?'

She knew he was changing the subject but she nodded anyway. 'Trevor Simpson's dealing with it. The fire people think the student left the gas on. There was very little left of the caravan or him. They were only able to confirm his identity from the dental records. A young lad of his age, such a shame. His parents must be devastated. I've always had a fear of fire; what a horrible way to die.'

'So, are you all right about me taking Sue out?'

'No, I'm not, Ray. Not one little bit. But I know you're going to do it anyway. So, we haven't had this conversation. You never told me a thing. And for God's sake don't let Halliday find out. That's the last thing you need. He would not be happy.'

'I've been thinking, if I buy Sue a drink or two, she may open up a bit. She may even change her story about being with Beth at the time of Harper's death. You know what I think about coincidences. If Sue's lying, the alcohol could make her more inclined to talk. She may let something slip. I still think Beth's our best bet as the driver. It's not like we've got any other viable suspects. It's got to be worth a try.'

Kesey lowered her eyebrows. 'Oh no, is that what this is really about? You're taking that unfortunate woman out to try to undermine Beth's alibi?'

'Well, that's not why I agreed at first. It was more shock that she'd asked me than anything else. But now that I think about it, these chances don't come along very often. Why not take full advantage?'

'That seems underhand even for you.'

Lewis grinned. 'Does that mean I can claim the evening on expenses?'

'No, it doesn't, Ray. Don't even think about it. The least you can do is buy the poor woman a meal. And do not put too much pressure on her. She's made her statement and is very likely fragile. There's every chance she told the truth. We've got nothing to suggest otherwise. The last thing she needs is you stamping all over her life with your size tens.'

35

Lewis had made an effort. He'd shaved for the second time that day, splashed on some cheap but inoffensive aftershave, donned an ill-fitting suit last worn at a friend's wedding some five years before, and had even polished his shoes, a rare event he usually reserved for Crown Court appearances. He was feeling strangely apprehensive as he drove through town a lot faster than was sensible, approaching the refuge a couple of minutes later than he'd initially planned. He acknowledged that he was less sure of himself than usual as he turned into Curzon Street. And he wanted to impress. There was no doubt on that score. He wanted to impress perhaps more than he should. The last thing he wanted was to be late. It wasn't the gentlemanly thing to do.

Lewis pulled up directly outside the refuge, half on and half off the curb to avoid causing an obstruction to other evening traffic. He adjusted his thinning hair in the rear-view mirror, spending a few seconds trying to hide a bald spot, before giving up on the idea as a lost cause. Who was he trying to kid? He was getting on a bit. There was no denying it. He looked old and worn down by life. What the hell did she see in him?

Lewis drove his self-deprecating thoughts from his mind as he pressed down on his car's horn three times in quick succession. He drummed his fingers on the steering wheel until Susan Johnson finally emerged through the high, steel security gate about five minutes later. Lewis thought that she looked spectacular in the light of a nearby street lamp. She was a good many years younger than him, and stunning in a figure-hugging skirt and jacket combo complemented by high-heeled shoes that couldn't help but get a middle-aged detective's pulse racing to a new and dangerous high. Lewis exited the car with surprising speed and agility for a man of his fleshy build. He hurried around to the passenger side on quick-moving feet, holding the door open for her to enter the car, with a fixed grin on his face that he couldn't hope to suppress.

He climbed into the driver's seat, and for the first time since courting his ex-wife many years before he felt a sudden surge of excitement at the idea of female company. Maybe he should forget about probing Sue for information. The job had made him cynical, suspicious of everyone. Why not enjoy a pleasant evening with an attractive younger woman who was so far out of his league. She seemed to like him for some inexplicable reason. Yes, make the most of it while he had the chance. It wasn't like it happened often. There was more to life than police work. He wasn't on duty now.

Lewis steered into the main road, signalling to his left and turning in the direction of the town centre, a short drive away.

'Where would you like to go, love? I thought maybe the Indian place in Merlin's Lane? They do a cracking curry and rice. Although, if you'd prefer somewhere else, that's fine with me. You only have to say. But wherever we go, it's my treat. I never let a lady pay.'

Sue checked her cherry-red lipstick in the vanity mirror.

'You're looking very handsome tonight, Raymond. Is that a new suit?'

Lewis wasn't quite speechless. But he struggled to say something that he thought even remotely sensible. He blurted out his reply. 'What, this old thing? No– no, it's... er... I've had it for ages.'

'And your aftershave, *very* sexy!'

This time he was lost for words.

'The curry house sounds perfect. I'm sure we're going to have a lovely evening together. I've been looking forward to it ever since you said yes to our date. I'm so very glad that you did.'

Lewis touched the brake as the traffic slowed in the road in front of them. 'Why me, love? Me of all people. I'm not exactly Brad Pitt. I've never been a looker. You could have your choice of blokes.'

'Don't be such a silly boy. You've got a lot going for you. I like you. Is that so hard to accept?'

Lewis couldn't quite believe his ears. It had been a very long time since a woman had complimented him, and never one as attractive as this. A part of him believed her words were genuine, but only a part. 'There's some CDs in the glovebox if you fancy a bit of music.'

Sue selected one and smiled. 'Oh, here we are, something nice and romantic. I love country music.'

Lewis was feeling very out of practice. How long had it been since his last first date? Thirty years maybe, or even longer. He decided he'd had enough of small talk. Perhaps she had too. Why not say something real? It may even impress her. 'I've been wondering how you're doing after that incident with Pearson? It can't have been a pleasant experience.'

'No, it wasn't. He's an evil man, so unlike yourself. What happened to him after he was dragged away in handcuffs?'

Lewis beeped the car's horn and waved on spotting a neighbour walking on by. 'What can I tell you? He was charged and released. He's already back on the streets.'

Sue's entire body tensed. 'Poor Sally was terrified. You should have seen the look on her face. The bastard should be locked up in a cell. He really scared me too.'

'It's a relatively minor offence. He didn't actually assault anyone. There's only so much we can do.'

Sue forced an unlikely smile as she reached out, patting his knee, allowing her hand to linger for a second or two. 'Well, I'm feeling a lot safer sitting here with a big strong man like you.'

Lewis was feeling even more out of his depth. He couldn't believe his luck. But he feared he'd screw things up at any moment. He hadn't had a love life for a very long time. And for the first time in years, he was telling himself a woman found him desirable. Not just any woman, but this beautiful woman with her long blonde hair, sky-blue eyes and shapely figure. It felt good. Better than good. It felt great. And talking about work had helped. Familiar ground.

'Are you sure the Indian's okay for you, love? Now's the time to say if it's not.'

Sue turned up the music's volume and smiled again, tapping her foot along to the melodic rhythm. 'As long as we're together I don't care where we go. I'm just glad to be out in town without feeling frightened. I can't tell you how much that means to me. You've made a girl very happy. Let's just enjoy ourselves. For tonight bastards like Pearson don't exist. Only good things happen to good people like you and me.'

'All right, love, the Indian it is.'

Lewis spotted an available parking place about halfway down King Street on the left, close to the cinema. As the unlikely couple walked across the one-way road and down Merlin's Lane towards the restaurant, Sue took the detective's hand in hers, holding it tightly as she told him how much she was looking forward to whatever the night would bring. Lewis had never felt more fortunate as he held open the restaurant door, allowing Sue to totter in on three-inch heels, which he thought made her legs look as if they went on forever. The detective glanced at her shapely bottom as he followed her into an atmospheric room decorated with warm, vibrant colours and layers of texture, a combination of which enticed diners to come in and get comfortable. Lewis chose a table for two, topped with a white cloth edged with small dangling balls. He pulled out an intricately hand-carved Indian chair to allow his date to sit first and then sat himself down opposite her, still not able to believe his good fortune.

Lewis looked at Sue and grinned as an attentive waiter dressed in smart scarlet and gold livery approached their table.

'Do you fancy a quick drink before we order food, love?'

Sue nodded as the waiter stood to wait. 'A glass of water would be lovely, thanks. I'm a real lightweight when it comes to alcohol.'

The detective's face fell. 'Aren't you going to have a real drink with me?'

'Oh, go on then. It is a special occasion. I'll have a glass of lager. I find it always goes well with spicy food, even when it's cold outside.'

'That's the spirit, let's make a night of it.'

'What about the car?'

'We can leave it where it is. I'll call a taxi.'

Lewis was close to finishing his third pint of strong beer by the time their first course arrived, onion bhajis for him and chicken pakora for her, accompanied by poppadoms and sweet mango chutney, the combined pleasant aroma of which filled the air to good effect. Sue was still on her first drink, having only sipped a small amount of cold lager from time to time when she felt she had no other option.

'Why don't you have another pint of beer, Raymond? You look as if you're enjoying it. I like to see a man appreciating a drink. It's so very manly.'

He was glad of the encouragement. It was so unlike the inevitable criticism dished out by his ex-wife in years gone by. It seemed Sue wanted him to have a good time. And what was wrong with that?

Sue used her foot to urgently push her bag a little further under the table on spotting the merest glint of a blade in the lamplight. 'I'm looking forward to my main course. I love biryani. How about you?'

'I always have vindaloo. I have done since I was a young man. I'm a creature of habit. The hotter, the better.'

She reached across the table to touch his hand. 'I like that. It makes you sound reliable. So unlike some of the men I've known in my life. I wish I'd met someone like you long ago. My life could have been so very different.'

He ordered himself a fourth pint of beer from the same immaculately dressed waiter who'd arrived with a hostess trolley laden with their next aromatic course.

'Shall we order a bottle of wine, Raymond? I rather fancy something fizzy.' She met his eyes as she ran her tongue over her top lip. 'Although I must warn you, I sometimes get rather naughty if I drink too much.'

She blew him a kiss as he ordered champagne, the most expensive bottle on the menu.

'Oh, that will be lovely, Raymond, thank you, you're so very kind. I do like a generous man.'

As the evening progressed, Sue fluttered her eyelids, laughed at his jokes, whether amusing or not, and encouraged him to drink at every possible opportunity, while carefully restricting her own alcohol intake. By the time dessert arrived about forty minutes later, Lewis was slurring his words.

'Raymond, I hope you don't mind me asking. Are you any closer to catching Harper's killer?'

'I... er... that's... er... that's not really something I can talk about, love.'

She leant forward, taking full advantage of her cleavage as she touched his face. 'Oh, come on, you can tell little old me. You don't still think that Beth had anything to do with it, do you?'

He burped on draining his glass. 'Um, yeah, maybe, I... er... I can't really say. It's– it's police business.'

'Have another glass of champagne, Raymond. Here, let me pour it for you. You're all fingers and thumbs. We're having such a lovely chat.'

He downed half the glass, burping for the second time before wiping his mouth with his free hand. There were yellow curry stains on his shirt and tie.

'Do you trust me, Raymond?'

He looked first at her lips, then at her boobs, and then at her lips again. Those full cherry-red lips he was so desperate to kiss. He was trying to figure out what to say, finally deciding that honesty was the most likely to impress. 'Well... er... I did– I did think you... er... were maybe lying for a time. But, I've got to know you better. We're friends now, so– so, I have to believe you.'

'Beth was telling the truth all along. You do understand that now, don't you? She had nothing to do with that man being run over in the road. Beth was telling the truth, and so was I.'

'Yeah, anything you say, love. You've– you've got lovely eyes. Have I told you that?'

'What does it matter who killed a nasty piece of work like Harper? They did the world a favour. That's what I think. Don't you agree?'

'Nobody – We... er... we all have to live by the law.'

'Drink your champagne, Raymond. Maybe when we finish here, we can go back to your place for a nightcap. You'd like that, wouldn't you, just me and you alone in the dark?'

Lewis couldn't empty has glass fast enough.

'Will you tell me a secret?'

He gave her a lopsided grin. 'What– what secret?'

'What would you do if you found out that Harper's killer was someone who did it for *all* the right reasons? Someone who wanted to prevent other innocent women and children being hurt by him. What would you do then?'

'What– what are you talking about? Do you– do you know something?'

She shook her head slowly, first one way and then the other. 'I'm not saying anything. I want to find out what *you* think. If you really liked me, you'd tell me your thoughts. Best friends don't keep secrets from each other. We are friends, aren't we?'

'I'd... er... I'd have to nick 'em, even if– even if I didn't want to.'

Sue's expression darkened. 'Oh, that's very disappointing, Raymond. I was hoping you'd say something very different.'

'It's the job, love. That's– that's the way it is. Shall we o-order a taxi? I'm– I'm feeling a bit pissed. The room, it's... er... it's starting to spin.'

Sue was reaching into her bag, searching for the small bottle of sedative liquid when the restaurant door suddenly opened. Kesey and Janet entered the room, Kesey taking the lead, dressed in knee-high winter boots, a warm coat and woolly hat pulled down low. The detective spotted Lewis almost immediately and made a beeline for the table. Lewis struggled to his feet to greet her, but he suddenly stumbled, falling heavily to the floor, colliding with a nearby table leg and sending two plated meals and a large carafe of mineral water crashing to the carpet.

Kesey used all her strength and weight to help him to his

feet while mumbling apologies to everyone in the vicinity. She took her sergeant's arm and marched him out into the cold, fresh night-time air. 'I wonder what the hell is wrong with you sometimes. I'm going to call you a cab and then I'm going to run that poor woman back to the refuge. You've ruined the evening for all of us. Jan is going to be fuming. And don't even think about trying to contact Sue again tonight. She's had enough of your crap. And so have I, in case you were wondering. You're a damned disgrace, Ray. I hope you're proud of yourself.'

36

The six women sat in a circle in the dimly lit cellar of Ivy's detached cottage, each with serious expressions on their faces as they waited for the proceedings to begin. Ivy was sat at the centre point of the room on a throne-like seat bought in a local auction house, with Sue immediately to one side of her and Karen Hoyle to the other. Louise, Kim and Beth formed the rest of the circle positioned opposite them.

Harry Smith, Beth's physical and psychological abuser, lay naked, drugged, bound and gagged in a far corner of the cellar, half-hidden under an old, bloodstained canvas tarpaulin with his bare legs sticking out. Sally was waiting in a first-floor bedroom, which like the cellar, had been soundproofed months before by two of the women, following the advice of online DIY videos.

Ivy rose to her feet at precisely 8pm, raising a clenched fist in the air as she met each of the women's eyes in turn and shouted, 'The Sisterhood!'

Each woman stood in turn, following Ivy's lead, calling out as she had before them, before returning to their seats. Ivy waited for the well-established protocol to end to her satisfaction before speaking again in ceremonious tones she thought best suited the solemnity of the proceedings. 'Welcome, ladies, welcome to this, the latest meeting of our beloved Sisterhood.'

All the attendees clapped and smiled, calling out enthusiastic words of thanks and encouragement before finally returning to silence.

Ivy waited for a few seconds before speaking again, her tone even more solemn now, the celebration over at least for the moment. 'I'm sure that I don't need to remind you all that everything that happens here must stay within these four walls. Nothing that is said or done in our name must ever be repeated. The continuation of our worthy quest depends on your continued integrity. Secrecy is everything.'

Each of the women began chanting in unison, their voices rising in harmony. 'Secrecy, secrecy, secrecy!'

Ivy beamed as the room finally returned to silence. 'Thank you, ladies. Your enthusiasm and dedication is appreciated, as always. It's an honour to be your leader.'

The group clapped again, for a little longer this time, eventually stopping when Ivy raised a hand, palm forward, fingers spread. 'Thank you again, ladies, but now to business. We have important matters to discuss.' She turned in her seat, facing the hospital social worker, who had a thin sheaf of papers resting on her lap. 'If you could hand out the agenda now, please, Karen, that would be most helpful.'

The social worker followed orders, handing each woman a single sheet of printed paper, in turn, starting with Ivy, who now spoke again, keen to move the meeting along as the seconds ticked by. She wasn't fond of late nights. Her bed was already calling despite the relatively early hour. 'As you can all see, there are three items on tonight's agenda. Item one is our usual update when I'll ask each of you, in turn, to share your recent actions on behalf of our glorious Sisterhood.

'Sue and Beth have been particularly active since our last meeting, and I feel sure their contributions will be fascinating.

'We'll then move on to welcome young Sally to the group. Something I'm sure you're all looking forward to immensely. It's always a great pleasure to bring another survivor under our protective wing.

'And then finally, as a climax to the ceremony, we'll move on to dispatch Beth's tormentor by lethal injection before going upstairs for refreshments. It's something we've only done once before *in situ*, so to speak. Not all of you have taken part. And I feel sure it will prove a rewarding experience. Sally will, of course, be asked to administer the deadly drug as an initial demonstration of her loyalty to our group. I would ask that you all give her every encouragement. I'm sure you'll remember your first time and how onerous the responsibility can feel, even without others looking on as in this case. It's going to be a big moment for her. We need to make it special.'

Ivy waited for the many whoops and claps of approval to subside. 'Kim has been kind enough to prepare some delicious sandwiches that we can all enjoy together at the end of the proceedings, and so I'm sure we'll all look forward to that. There's also cake as always, although I've also made a large creamy rice pudding as a special treat. Sue tells me it's Sally's favourite sweet dessert. And so it seemed appropriate.'

The room erupted in cheers.

'You'll no doubt be pleased to hear that I've decided that we should leave the disposal of the tormentor's corpse until tomorrow. Dismemberment took significantly longer than expected the last time, and so it seems ill-advised to start the process tonight, particularly when we have refreshments to share and enjoy. Sue, if you could join me in the morning, we can do the necessary together. I'm sure we can manage the process perfectly well if we use the correct equipment. The body parts can then stay where they are to await later disposal in the back garden after dark. That, regrettably, will involve some digging. Louise, if you could help me with that. I think you'll find it's your turn. I'll speak to you later to agree a time. The roses will be appreciative if nothing else.'

The cellar was filled with happy, lively chatter as the women clapped their enthusiastic approval. Beth, while appearing less enthused, clapped along with the rest.

'Thank you, ladies, thank you once more. Your support for our work is to your credit. But if you could all settle down now, I'll ask Sue to address us. She's been a very busy girl recently, and so I'm sure she'll have lots to share.'

Sue stood to the sound of her name. She spent the next ten minutes recounting her exploits in Cardiff while the women sat and listened, asking pertinent questions and indicating their approval when they thought it appropriate. Sue briefly considered sharing the details of Mr B's recent death, but she quickly dismissed the idea out of hand. That particular killing hadn't been sanctioned by Ivy, and so silence on the matter seemed advisable.

Beth spoke once Sue had finished her presentation, followed by each of the other women, who had less to say but were still keen to contribute. Beth glanced towards Harry Smith repeatedly as she gave her talk. She appeared close to tears at one point, but she made no reference to her ex-partner at any stage. Ivy suggested they stop for a brief comfort break at just before nine, stating that Sally would be brought down for the initiation ceremony once they'd all returned to the cellar. There was an air of excitement as each of the women climbed the ten cold grey concrete steps towards the toilet facilities on the ground floor.

Sue knocked on the bedroom door before entering the eggshell-blue painted room to find Sally curled up and asleep on the double bed. Sue gently shook Sally awake with a warm smile on her beautiful face. 'It's time, Sally. This is it. You're going to be a member of The Sisterhood. Isn't that wonderful?'

Sally yawned and stretched, her ribs still a little painful as she slid off the bed, standing with Sue's hand in hers. 'Is it that time already?'

Sue nodded. 'Are you excited?'

'I'm a bit nervous, to be honest.'

Sue hugged her. 'We're all friends here. Everything is going to be fine. Are you ready?'

'As ready as I'll ever be.'

'Come on then, down we go. Try to relax, it's going to be brilliant.'

Sue led Sally down the stairs, across the lounge, and then finally down into the cellar, where everyone was waiting in a state of high anticipation. Sue entered first, followed by Sally, who repeatedly blinked as her eyes adjusted to the dim light. All the women stood to call out their enthusiastic greetings, led by Ivy, who took the lead, orchestrating the welcome as she had for all new members before.

'Welcome, Sally! Welcome to your first meeting of our esteemed Sisterhood. You will be reborn, one of us, a tigress, the world will hear you roar. Sit, ladies, sit, all but you, Sally. You should remain standing. This is your moment in the spotlight, the greatest moment of your life. Nothing will be the same from here on in.'

Sally hadn't seen the bound and unconscious man up to that point, but now as she stood at the centre of the circle with each of the other women seated around her, she asked herself how she hadn't spotted him as soon as she'd entered the room. Sally felt a cold shiver run down her spine. She wanted to say something, to ask the obvious questions, even to go to his aid. But instead, she just stood there, shivering, frozen in indecision, unable to do or even say anything at all.

Ivy walked towards Sally, standing immediately in front of her with a hand resting on her shoulder. 'What you're about to say is an unbreakable oath. A solemn promise never to be sullied. You'll now repeat everything I say loudly and clearly enough for all to hear. Think about the words as you pronounce them, appreciate their importance, they'll become a part of you. Are you ready to begin?'

Sally looked at anything but the naked man as she nodded once. She drove his image from her mind.

'Say this after me... I, Sally, swear total loyalty to my sisters.'

Sally repeated the words in a faltering voice.

'Say it again, Sally, louder and with more conviction this time. We all need to hear your wonderful words.'

Sally repeated herself, louder this time, as she looked at each woman in turn.

Ivy continued. 'That's excellent, very well done, Sally, you're doing well. Now say after me... My sisters are my family. They matter above all others. I swear faithfulness to The Sisterhood on pain of death. My duty is only to the group.'

Sally's eyes moistened. 'Could you say it again, please?'

Ivy repeated herself, more slowly this time, allowing Sally to reproduce each sentence in turn until the entire oath was finally complete. The room erupted in boisterous applause the second Sally finished her final sentence. Each woman stood, rushing toward her and hugging her while uttering words of warm congratulation. This continued for almost five minutes until the women finally returned to their seats, leaving Sally standing alone at the centre of the circle. Ivy walked slowly towards her, handing her a syringe filled with a clear liquid. Sally stared at it as she took it in hand, and then met Ivy's gaze, waiting for her to speak, as she inevitably would.

'I need you to listen to me very carefully, Sally. I want you to approach the tormentor over there in that dark corner, I want you to stab that needle deep into his thigh, and then I want you to press down the plunger, administering the medication he so very badly needs. His evil is beyond cure. Only death will achieve the desired outcome. And so you must put an end to his destructive life. When you do that one good thing you cement your membership of The Sisterhood. You will be one of us now and forever. There is no greater honour.'

Sally turned away, walking slowly toward the man, who had started groaning quietly in his chemically induced sleep. Ivy began chanting, 'Sally, Sally, Sally!' as the young girl approached the man and knelt at his side. Everyone joined in, 'Do it, do it, do it!' as Sally poised the needle above the man's bare leg. And then they all erupted, calling out louder than at any prior point of the evening as Sally plunged the needle deep into his flesh. 'Sally, Sally, Sally! All power to The Sisterhood! You are one of us! The world has heard you roar!'

37

Kesey had just pulled up in the West Wales Police HQ car park when she spotted Lewis trudging up the steps into the modernist building. She switched off her car's engine, pulled up the handbrake and hurried after him, jogging across the wet tarmacadam with gradually increasing pace as the rain began to fall.

She said a quick 'Good morning' to Sandra on the front desk, as she headed for the lift in the sure knowledge that Lewis was unlikely to use the stairs. Kesey called out to her sergeant just as the lift doors were opening, but he stepped in anyway, as if he hadn't heard her at all. By the time she finally caught up with him in his shared office, she was both slightly out of breath and more irritated than she'd been in quite some time. Lewis was alone in the room when she pushed open the door. He looked tired, unshaven, and, if anything, a little heavier than when she'd last seen him only three days before.

'Nice of you to finally make an appearance. Have you thought about actually answering your phone? I've left message after message. Where the hell have you been?'

Lewis averted his eyes to the wall, avoiding her accusing gaze. 'I took a couple of days of sick leave.'

She approached his desk. 'I'm very well aware of that, thank you, Ray. But why you couldn't respond to my texts is still a mystery. I know you saw them. Perhaps you'd like to enlighten me.'

He bent down to switch on the kettle. 'Fancy a coffee?'

'Just answer the damned question. You are winding me right up.'

He massaged his forehead. 'I've been thinking about that night in the Indian.'

'Oh, so you do remember it, then? I thought you might have been too pissed to recall anything at all. You made a serious prat of yourself. I hope you realise that. You're a grown man, not some stupid teenager. What the hell was going on in your head?'

He spooned coffee into two mugs before adding powdered milk. 'I thought I was in control of the situation. I thought it was me orchestrating events. But now I'm not so sure.'

'Surely you're not trying to make excuses for the horrendous state you were in? I was there. I saw you. I had to lift you off the damned floor. You could hardly string a sentence together.'

He went to hand Kesey her mug, but withdrew it, placing it on his desk when she didn't accept it. 'I really think Sue may have been playing me.'

Kesey looked at him with a sneer. 'Oh, come off it, Ray, no more excuses. Take responsibility for yourself. I've never heard anything more pathetic in my life.'

He threw a hand in the air. 'You're not listening to me, boss. I know I made an idiot of myself. I know I'm more than capable of doing that all by myself after a few drinks too many. But I think there was more to it this time.'

Kesey pulled up a chair, a little calmer now, but still bristling.

'Come on, tell me what you're thinking. And this had better be good. Jan still hasn't forgiven you for ruining our night. I was already in the doghouse for missing her birthday without you making it worse.'

'Sue asked me out, yeah. Why would she do that? A good-looking young woman like her. It's not like she's short of male attention. I bet blokes are falling over themselves.'

She grinned for the first time that morning. 'Beats me?'

'No, I'm being serious, Laura. I think she had an ulterior motive. It wasn't just a night out. She was fishing for information.'

Kesey finally picked up her mug, but she didn't drink. 'If this is some ridiculous attempt to justify the state you were in, I'm not impressed.'

'I'm not making excuses. I drank too much, I'm a grown-up, that's down to me. But Sue played her part. She repeatedly encouraged me to drink while remaining sober herself. I only realised that the next day. She hardly touched a drop. And she didn't start asking me about the job until I'd had a few. I think that was deliberate. I think she knew exactly what she was doing.'

'The woman talked to you about work. Big deal, it's all you've got in common. What else is she going to talk to you about?'

Lewis slurped his hot drink, adding another sugar before drinking again. 'You're not getting what I'm telling you. Her questions about our investigation were the whole point of the evening. That's why she rang me, that's why she asked me out, that's why she tarted herself up, flirted with me, and laughed at my jokes. She took me for a mug. I'm increasingly thinking she's not what she seems.'

'Even if it's true, none of what you've said means she's lied to us at any point of the investigation.'

Lewis looked up at the ceiling. 'No, but it tells me she *may* have. I've always had my doubts, you know that, but they're growing. I think we at least need to check out her background.'

'I've checked. She hasn't got a record. It's something I've done for all the women.'

'Shit!'

'Why's this bothering you so much, is it a pride thing?'

'What if I meet with her again? I could apologise. Offer to buy her a coffee one afternoon. She asked me how I'd feel if Harper's killer did it for all the right reasons. I was too pissed to read anything into it at the time. But now I'm thinking, was that some kind of convoluted admission that either she killed him herself, or she knows who did.'

Kesey made a face. 'That is one hell of a leap.'

'Just let me talk to her, boss. If I'm right, then great, and if I'm not, what have we lost? We just move on as if the meeting never happened.'

A look of recognition suddenly dawned on Kesey's face. 'Oh, I get it. You've already arranged all this, haven't you? It's a done deal.'

'I'm meeting her at Beth's café next Saturday evening. You know, the small veggie place in Merlin's Lane. There's an open mic thing on. It's the first day Sue can get a babysitter.'

Kesey was quiet for a few seconds before finally speaking. 'I can't believe I'm actually saying this, but go ahead, see if there's anything to find out. But do not under any circumstances touch any alcohol. Not a *drop*! You've embarrassed me enough for one lifetime.'

38

Kim first saw Michael Pearson leaning against the bar in the Riverbank Nightclub at just after 11pm. It was one of his regular haunts. A favourite watering hole he visited almost every Friday night, to drink too much alcohol, snort cocaine, and hit on any woman in his vicinity. Kim intended to take full advantage of those facts as she slowly approached him with her best smile on her pretty face. Ivy had made her expectations perfectly clear. The system had failed. Pearson had to die in the interests of justice. And that was down to her. The Sisterhood would expect no less.

'Fancy a dance?'

Pearson glanced behind him, thinking the glamorous young woman in the short black leather skirt and tight blue top may be speaking to somebody else. 'Are you talking to me, darling?'

Kim took Pearson's hand in hers, leading him towards an almost empty dance floor without saying another word. There was a glow about her as she began dancing, radiating seductive passion and pleasure with every movement of her slim body. She began twerking as the pounding music got gradually faster, thrusting her hips provocatively in a low stance, shaking her bottom while balanced on her stilettos. Pearson just stood there and watched with a wide grin as the young woman moved around him. He reached out, trying to touch her repeatedly, but she moved away with sinewy grace, staying just out of his reach until a new track began.

Kim noticed that Pearson was already worse for drink as she retook his hand, leading him back towards the bar. And that, she decided, was a good thing. It made her task more manageable. She could get it over with more quickly. There would be less effort involved.

Kim looked into Pearson's drunken eyes, pouting. 'Aren't you going to buy me a drink, then? You shouldn't keep a girl waiting.'

He lurched forward, trying to kiss her mouth, but she moved away just in time. 'Drinks first, sex later, you need to be patient.'

She could see the repressed anger in his face as he glared back at her. He was trying to hide it, but it was there.

'What are you going to have?'

She shouted above the music, waves of sound vibrating around the darkened space. 'I'll have a gin and tonic unless you've got anything more interesting to offer.'

He screwed up his face, placing his mouth close to her ear. 'What have you got in mind?'

Kim raised her manicured fingers to her button nose, touching each nostril in turn and sniffing.

A look of understanding crossed Pearson's face. 'What do I get in return?'

'I've got some crazy stuff that will blow your mind. Use it, and you'll be able to fuck all night.'

His eyes lit up. 'I usually use the disabled bog. There's more room. And the bouncers won't bother us. I tip them a few quid at the start of the night.'

Kim touched his hip. 'What are we waiting for?'

Pearson entered the cubicle first with Kim following soon

after. The drug stung the lining of her nose as she sniffed it in for the first time in her life. She sneezed, glad to expel as much the white powder as possible, and then encouraged him to indulge his addiction, rather than take more herself.

Pearson slumped down on the toilet seat. 'That's a great buzz.'

Kim took a plastic syringe from her pineapple-yellow clutch bag. 'If you think that's good, you should try this stuff. It's the best high I've ever experienced. Absolutely *amazing*! Get ready for take-off. It's going to be a crazy ride.'

Pearson watched as Kim took a glass vial from her bag, breaking off its top with a snap that could only just be heard above the sound of a rhythmic dance track. She attached a needle to the syringe, discarded the wrapper in the toilet bowl, inserted the needle precisely through the mouth of the vial, and slowly drew the clear liquid into the syringe chamber. Finally, she pressed the plunger gently with her thumb, forcing out the air, until a tiny drop of the sedative liquid squirted from the tip of the needle. She was ready. She reached out with her free hand, touching his chest, and then handed him the syringe. She gave him her most seductive look and knew he was succumbing. 'You first, you won't be sorry, trust me. You're going to have the hottest night of your life.'

Pearson stood, took off his designer jacket, rolled up his shirtsleeve, pumped his arm repeatedly, and then carefully inserted the point of the sharp needle into a prominent vein located in the triangular area inside his elbow. Within seconds his eyes clouded. He lost balance, staggering, bouncing against a wall and dropping the syringe to the tiled floor. 'What the fuck have I just used?'

Kim hurriedly returned the syringe to her bag for later disposal somewhere she felt confident it wouldn't be found. She took Pearson's hand, leading him down a dim corridor towards the dance floor and exit beyond. 'Come on, let's get you out into the fresh air. And then we can go back to your place. You do want that, don't you, Michael? You are man enough, aren't you?'

'How the fuck do you know my name?'

What to say? 'Don't you remember telling me at the bar?'

'No!'

'Well, you did.'

Pearson was looking increasingly confused as she led him past the two black-clad doormen standing at the club's entrance, and out into the quiet night-time street, which ran along the riverbank in the direction of town. 'Come on, Michael. My car's only a couple of minutes' walk away. Keep going, you can do it, one step at a time. It's going to be worth it.'

He staggered and nearly fell. 'What the fuck was that stuff?'

Kim guided him across the road to where a low wall separated the one-way street from the tidal river. There was a four- to five-foot drop into the swirling brown mix of fresh and saltwater. She hurried him along as he faltered, rounding a bend and out of sight of the bouncers. 'Are you okay, Michael? It's not much further.'

'I think I'm going to puke.'

Kim pushed him gently along, manoeuvring him towards the low wall, which reached his mid-thighs. She stood behind him as he gagged, vomiting into the swirling water. She looked around her, ensuring there were no witnesses before using all her weight and strength to shove him. Pearson tumbled over the wall head first, turning as he fell and hitting the dark water head first under a second later.

He flailed about for what seemed like an age before the outgoing tide swept him away from the wall. And then his head went under for the first time. He tried to swim, but he was too weak, the water too cold, the current too strong. As his head bobbed under for the second time, Kim started shouting for help. She screamed louder and louder, tears running down her face until a large and muscular bouncer with a smoothly shaved head arrived at her side.

'What the fuck's happened?'

Kim looked at the muscly stranger with feverish, over-bright eyes filled with tears. She'd never felt better. 'He was pissed, he was puking, he– he fell in.'

'Who did? Who are you talking about?'

She pointed towards the river with a quivering hand. 'The guy I met in the club. He fell– he fell in the river. He– he disappeared under the water. I don't think he could swim.'

The bouncer looked out on the dark water, straining his eyes, scanning the surface from one bank to the other. But there was no-one to see. Pearson's body had been swept away in the direction of the sea. 'It's too late, he's gone.'

Kim was bawling now, seemingly in a state of great distress. She'd once been a member of an amateur dramatics group and was putting those skills to good use. 'Phone for help. For God's sake, call for help!'

The bouncer dialled before raising his mobile to his face. 'Police, please, and an ambulance, I need an ambulance.'

Kim sat herself down on the low wall as the doorman provided the call handler with the required information, rushing his words. She looked out on the fast-flowing water, still in tears, and silently celebrated Pearson's death as she waited for the emergency services to arrive.

39

Lewis was already seated in a quiet spot at the far side of the bar behind a worn-out pool table when Kesey entered the Caerystwyth Rugby Club a few minutes after two the following afternoon. Her sergeant seemed unaware of her arrival, sitting as he was with a pint in hand, having chosen a seat with a good view of the barmaid and her overflowing blouse. There were three empty crisp packets on the table in front of him.

Kesey ordered coffee before approaching Lewis, deliberately positioning herself between him and the bar before settling in her seat. She blew her steaming beverage to cool it, drank a small amount, and then placed her cup back on its matching saucer.

'What am I doing here, Ray?'

He slurped his beer, draining almost half the glass. 'I just wanted an informal chat without the danger of anyone else sticking their nose in.'

'Couldn't we have done that at the station?'

'I'm comfortable here. This place helps me think.'

Kesey drew breath, releasing it before speaking. She pointed at his glass. 'How many have you had?'

'I haven't long been here. Just the one.'

She doubted he'd told her the truth. 'Are you all right, Ray? You don't seem yourself.'

'It's just this fucking case. It's doing my head in. I can't help feeling we've been had.'

'What are you talking about now?'

Lewis drained his glass, pushing it aside rather than ordering another pint. 'Did you hear about Pearson?'

She nodded. 'Yeah, they fished him out of the estuary in Llansteffan this morning.'

'Don't you think it's strange?'

'Don't I think what's strange?'

'We had Harper's death, then Garvey's, and now Pearson's, all in a short time. And I know what you're going to say, Garvey was killed in Cardiff and Pearson's death looks like an accident. But was it? How sure can we be? You've got to admit it's one hell of a coincidence. Three local men dead in a matter of days, all with links to the same domestic violence refuge. I've said it before, and I'll say it again. I don't like it. Something is going on. It's too much of a coincidence for me.'

Kesey sipped her coffee and, unusual for her, on finding it too bitter added half a sachet of sugar. 'What is it with you, Ray? You drive me to distraction sometimes. Think about what you're saying before jumping to any more conclusions. We've got one guy run over by a car, one killed seventy plus miles away in a frenzied knife attack, and one who fell in the river when pissed and out of his head on cocaine. That's three *very* different deaths, two murders with drastically different MOs and what looks like a tragic accident witnessed by a woman who'd only met Pearson half an hour or so before he died. It all happened in a public area, albeit quiet at the time, and she even called for help, loud enough to be heard outside the club. It's a low wall. An accident waiting to happen. The bouncer was on the scene in two minutes maximum. He described Kim Garvey as being extremely distressed. She urgently asked him to summon help. Would she do all that if she'd just pushed Pearson into the water?'

'She may have.'

'Well, I guess there's always that possibility. But it seems *highly* unlikely to me. If she killed him, why not slope off and say nothing at all? There was no-one else about. Kim could have disappeared into the night without anyone to stop her. Surely that's what a guilty person would do.'

Lewis shrugged his big shoulders. 'Maybe she's cleverer than that. She must have known she'd been seen with Pearson in the club. She's a local girl. Someone would have recognised her. And anyway, they'd have been seen together on the club's security cameras. If Kim did push him in, hanging about and yelling for help would have been a great way of getting away with it. All she'd have had to do is wait just long enough for Pearson to drown before shouting out. Maybe she's a good actress. She could be taking us for mugs.'

'What, like you claim Sue was, you mean? You're starting to sound ridiculous. You're in the realms of fantasy. Surely you're not still trying to suggest there's some kind of mass female conspiracy, are you?'

'I could be.'

Kesey held her hands out wide. 'And have you got any evidence to back this theory? Anything at all, other than wild conjecture?'

He looked away without responding to the provocation.

'And don't even think about talking about your gut feelings.

Feelings aren't evidence. Can you say anything at all to support this notion that the deaths are linked? Or is it just some crazy hypothesis you can't back up with proof or even logical reasoning? And that was a rhetorical question, by the way. I know the answer already. If you had anything worth saying, I'd have heard about it long before now.'

Lewis tore up a sodden beer mat, releasing pent up energy. 'I'm thinking of calling on Ivy for a chat before meeting Sue this evening.'

'What on earth for? What are you hoping to gain?'

'I'll talk to her as an old friend, at her place, off the record. Maybe she shares some of my suspicions. Perhaps she thinks there's something strange going on involving some of the women with links to the refuge. I'll tell her what I'm suspecting and ask her outright if she thinks there's any possibility I'm right. She may say yes. She may say no. But either way, we haven't lost anything. It may even give us a break.'

'Is that really the best you've got?'

He scratched an eyebrow. 'Look, boss, support me in doing this one thing. I don't think that's too much to ask. If it doesn't get us anywhere, I'll let it go. I'd admit I'm wrong.'

She sighed loudly enough to be heard by the barmaid on the other side of the room. 'Okay, go ahead, do what you feel you have to do. I know you won't shut up about it otherwise. But I do *not* want you putting any undue pressure on the woman. I know what you're like. If you're doing this, it's on that one condition. Ivy provides an invaluable service in this town. I don't want her upset. Are we agreed?'

'Yeah, all right, not a problem.'

'My own feeling is that if Ivy had any concerns, any at all, she'd have already told us all about them. She wouldn't keep them to herself, that's not her style.'

Lewis rose stiffly to his feet, still not persuaded. 'I'll let you know if I find out anything useful.'

Kesey drained her coffee cup, preparing to leave. 'You do that, Ray. But only ring me in the unlikely event that it's something important. If not, we'll talk on Monday. Jan's parents are staying for a couple of days. I'm trying to be the good wife. The last thing I want is to upset her again.'

40

Lewis sat in Ivy's comfortable lounge, sipping sweet tea from a floral cup and happily eating a second large slice of chocolate cake topped with rich fondant icing. His tie was pulled loose, and there were sticky crumbs over his chin and shirt-front as he lazed back in his seat, sinking into the soft cotton cushion. Ivy waited for him to finally stop eating before looking into his tired eyes and speaking for the first time in almost a minute.

'As nice as it is to see you again, Raymond, I can't help wondering why you're here. You don't visit for years, and now here you are again for the second time in a matter of days. What's going on?'

'Did you hear about Pearson's death?'

She nodded. 'Yes, he drowned. I can't say I'm sorry. He made young Sally's life a misery. She's been terrified since his release from prison. Perhaps now she can get on with her life.'

'Yeah, the man was a menace. I won't mourn his death, but it got me thinking.'

She tensed, fingering her bead necklace for a second or two before speaking again. 'Tell me more.'

'First, Harper died, then Garvey, and now Pearson, all in quick succession. You're probably going to think I'm crazy for even asking this, but have you ever wondered if any of the women linked to the refuge played any part in their deaths?'

She gave a little laugh. 'My girls? That's the most ridiculous thing I've ever heard.'

'What, you've never even wondered, not even once?'

She appeared more serious now, her smile becoming a frown. 'Have you been working too hard, Raymond? Perhaps it's time for a break. It's not wise to overdo things at your age. Has anyone ever told you that?'

He wasn't ready to let it go. 'Three deaths, all linked to the refuge. Why not one or more of the women? The system failed them. We know Kim was there when Pearson died. They could be working together. Taking matters into their own hands. I think it's a real possibility.'

'Have you any evidence?'

'I'll find the truth. I almost always do.'

Ivy cut him a third slice of cake. 'And what would you think if your intuitions turned out to be correct? Where would your sympathies lie? Purely conjecture, you understand. I'm not for a second suggesting that's what's actually happened. It's a theoretical question, nothing more. I'd be interested to know your thoughts.'

For the first time, Lewis thought he might be getting somewhere. 'No-one is beyond the law, not me, not you, and not your girls. If any of them are guilty, I'd understand, I'd sympathise, really I would. But I couldn't turn a blind eye. That would make a mockery of my role.'

Ivy stood, looking down at him with her hands linked behind her back. 'And would the guilty go to prison?'

'Yeah, they would, probably for a very long time.'

She looked away. 'I've got some lovely rhubarb wine I'd like you to sample. I made it myself. I'd value your opinion.'

His frustration couldn't have been more obvious. 'I'm driving.'

'You'd be very welcome to stop for a meal. I've got a spare bedroom. We could make a night of it. For old times if nothing else.'

Lewis scratched at his temple, grimacing. 'It's a nice idea. But I'm... er... I'm meeting Sue in town. It's all arranged.'

'Another time then, but one glass isn't going to do you any harm. Maybe then we can talk some more about your investigative theories. There may be more to it than I first thought.'

All of a sudden Lewis was feeling a lot more hopeful. It seemed his visit may not be a waste of time, after all. He was keen to know more. 'Yeah, go on then, why not? But it will have to be the one glass, no more than that.'

'That's the spirit; you won't be disappointed. It's an old recipe passed down from my grandmother. It's rather special.'

'If it's half as good as your cakes I'm in for a treat.'

Ivy disappeared into the kitchen, returning a minute or two later with a wine glass in each hand. Each was filled almost to the brim with a pinky-red liquid. She handed Lewis the glass in her right hand before settling back in her seat with the other. 'Drink away, drink away, Raymond. I'd love to know your thoughts.'

Lewis raised the wine glass to his mouth and drank. He thought the wine odd, not at all to his tastes, but he was never going to say that, not here, not now. He felt sure things were starting to go his way. He wanted to keep Ivy onside at almost any cost. She seemed more relaxed all of a sudden. More likely to talk openly. More likely to let something slip. He sipped the unpleasant drink again and then decided to down it in one. Why not get it over with as quickly as possible? He tilted his head back and drank. *There, gone.* He placed his empty glass on the low table. 'That was delicious, Ivy, really top-notch.'

'I can't persuade you to have another glass?'

He shook his head. 'No, I'd better not. Better safe than sorry. You know what it's like. I only wish I wasn't driving.'

They continued talking for a few minutes more. Lewis attempting to focus on the investigation and Ivy repeatedly retuning the conversation to the home-made wine.

'Are you sure I can't persuade you to have another glass?'

'No, like I said, I'm driving.'

'I've got a few more bottles keeping cool in the cellar. I'd love you to take one away with you. Come on. You can bring some up for me. I struggle with the steps these days. Age doesn't come alone.'

Lewis was already feeling a little unsteady as he stood. He shifted his weight from one foot to the other, regaining his balance as Ivy pointed towards the cellar door at the other side of the room close to the kitchen. 'That's it, Raymond, the cellar's over there, not far, open the door and go down the steps for me, there's a good lad. You can't miss the wine, there's a wooden crate on the right against the wall close to the tarpaulin.'

Lewis yawned as Ivy followed him across the room in the direction of the cellar door. He stood on the edge of the first grey concrete step looking down into the gloom, asking himself why he felt so very dizzy.

'That's it, Raymond, there's a light switch on the wall to your left. That's it, a little further. Down you go.'

As Lewis leaned forward, running the palm of his open hand over the uneven wall in search of the switch, Ivy shoved him hard, sending him tumbling down the steps and crashing to the cellar floor, where his head cracked violently against the concrete. He lay there moaning incoherently, drifting in and out of consciousness, as Ivy made her way down the steps towards him.

Lewis didn't come around for almost three hours when he found himself naked, bloody, bound and gagged, still lying on the unforgiving concrete. He opened his eyes, staring into the darkness, but seeing nothing at all. His head was pounding. His body was aching. And he was shivering uncontrollably. For the first time in a very long time, Lewis was scared. He struggled to the point of exhaustion but couldn't free himself. It was the lowest point of his life.

41

The women of The Sisterhood were back in the cellar, seated in their prior positions, only days after their previous meeting. Sally had been allocated a chair immediately to the right of Sue. She moved her seat a little closer when she thought no-one was watching, enabling her to reach out to intermittently hold Sue's reassuring hand when the mood took her. Sally found herself struggling with the whole experience, memories of her previous visit still raw.

Lewis was lying just a few feet behind her, still naked, bound and gagged, as Smith had been before him. Sally glanced around at one point, noticing that his troubled eyes were darting from one woman to the next, trying to meet their gaze, attempting to gain their attention, but it was as if they didn't see him at all. As if he was a non-person. As if he was invisible to everyone but her.

The women opposite the fat detective just sat and talked, their combined voices filling the crypt-like space with lively sound. Ivy allowed them to all to converse for a few minutes more before finally raising a hand to silence them. Sally hadn't said a word. She'd just sat and stared in silence, trying to drive her growing misgivings from her mind.

'Welcome, ladies, it's good to see you all again. I'm sorry to have had to call you back here so soon. Thank you for arriving so very promptly. It's to your credit as always. Your dedication never fails to impress.'

She pointed towards Lewis, who was once again attempting to free himself from his secure bindings with little if any hope of success. 'As you can all see, we have an important matter to discuss. An unexpected development that is far too significant to ignore.' Ivy punched the air at this point. 'All power to The Sisterhood!'

The women called out in unison, 'The Sisterhood!' Sally joined in, but with less enthusiasm than the others. She felt she had to.

Ivy continued, 'For those of you who don't recognise our unanticipated guest, I'd like to introduce you to Detective Sergeant Raymond Lewis of the West Wales Police Force. Raymond is a man I've known for quite some time, and unlike the cellar's previous guests, he is not, as far as I am aware, an abuser of women or children. In fact, to the contrary, I believe he has successfully investigated several cases involving predatory males over the years, which I feel certain we would all applaud in any other circumstances. He does, however, now pose a significant risk to our continued work, and therein lies the problem.'

Ivy cleared her throat before speaking again, her voice a little hoarse. 'It was clear from my discussions with him earlier today that he was getting far too close to the truth. He was like a dog with a bone, not willing to let the subject drop, asking awkward questions, sticking his interfering snout in where it didn't belong. That, I'm sure you'll agree, could not be allowed to continue. Something had to be done. And so, here he is in our secret space, an unwelcome invader in our midst. A snake in the grass.'

Ivy allowed a brief time for the resulting heated chatter to subside before raising a hand for the second time. 'That's enough conversation for now, please, ladies, I need you to listen to what I have to say next *very* carefully. My throat is a little sore. I don't wish to repeat myself.'

No-one said another word. They were silent in an instant. Only Lewis could be heard, as he sucked in the fetid air through his nose, his mouth still tightly bound.

'I didn't think it appropriate for me to decide on a course of action alone as I sometimes have in the past given the unique nature of our problem. We've never chosen to execute a non-abuser before. That would be a first for our group. An onerous responsibility, therefore, rests on all your shoulders. I am going to put Raymond's destiny to the vote. The majority will decide.

'I would remind you all, however, that if allowed to live, short of keeping him a prisoner forever, Sergeant Lewis will bring an inevitable end to our worthy work. I, for one, do not believe that should be allowed to happen. I suggest we now stop for refreshments, giving us all time to reflect on what we wish to do. We will reconvene here in twenty minutes precisely, at which time each of us will cast a vote either for the disbanding of our Sisterhood, or the execution of one man. I know what I'll be voting for. Tea, coffee and snacks will be available upstairs. And please feel free to speak to me for further guidance if you so wish. This is a crucial moment in our group's history. What we decided today will define our future.'

Sally hurried after Sue as the women climbed the stairs towards the sitting room. She tugged Sue's arm at one point, speaking directly into her ear. 'He hasn't done anything, Sue. He's not like the bastards who hurt us.'

Sue led Sally into the sitting room, and then the quieter hallway, where she closed the door. Sue stood immediately in front of Sally, close to the front door, their noses almost touching. 'You heard what Ivy said. The pig stuck his nose in. He shouldn't have come here. If he dies, that's his fault. That's down to *him*, not us. We've got to do the right thing. We've got to stay strong. Not for ourselves, but for The Sisterhood. Nothing matters more.'

Sally thought she might start weeping at any second. She could feel the tears welling up inside her. She wanted to be anywhere else, anywhere but there. 'But– but you know him. He– he came to the refuge. You said he was all right, a bit of prat but harmless. That's how you described him. And Ivy knows him too. She said he's a decent man, a force for good.'

'You've got to toughen up, Sally. Stop your blubbing. You're one of us now, a sister. That changes everything. Doing the right thing isn't always easy, not for everyone. But we've got to do it. There's no other choice.'

Sally looked at Sue with pleading eyes, her gut twisting with the fear of it all. She'd never felt more conflicted, never so desperate. She rushed her words. 'We could let him go. We could– we could make him promise never to say anything in return for his life. Why– why don't we do that?'

Sue gripped each of Sally's shoulders and shook her. 'Listen to yourself, girl. What the fuck are you saying? The pig's got to die. We can make it as painless as possible. He doesn't need to suffer any more than necessary. But he *has* got to go. We can't keep him down there forever. Face facts. Execution is the only viable choice.'

'But– but...'

Sue shook her again, more vigorously this time. 'It's time to shut up, Sally. Don't even think about voting to let the pig live. That wouldn't go down well with the rest of us. You'd be the only one. And Ivy may even decide that *you're* a danger to our group.

Things could get well out of hand. Do you want to be the next one to die? *Do you? Do you?'*

Sally's face was ashen. 'What– what, m-me? You think...'

'*Yes*, a million times, *yes!* We're going to go into the lounge. You're going to drink some tea, and eat a sandwich, and put a smile on your face, and then we're going to go back down into the cellar together, where you'll vote for the pig to die. Tell me you understand. I need to hear you say it. If you can't do that for me, I'm giving up on you. You're on your own.'

Sally was weeping now, the tears welling in her eyes and running down her face. 'All right, I'll– I'll do it. I... er... I know you're right. It's just that I've been having n-nightmares after– after the last time. I keep– I keep seeing that man sitting on the end of my bed once the lights go out. He stares at me. I don't know if he's real.'

Sue stepped back, slapping Sally's face hard, leaving a red, raised mark on her pale skin. 'Pull yourself together, girl. You're running out of time. I'm losing patience. This is your last chance. Get your act together, or I'm done with you.'

'I'm sorry, I'm ready, I'll do it, but I need to use the toilet first. It's– it's getting urgent.'

Sue's body relaxed slightly, the tension leaving her. 'Splash some water on your face when you're in there. Freshen yourself up. I'm trying to help you here. You look like crap.'

Sally forced an unlikely gap-toothed smile that she hoped would mask her growing anxiety. 'I will, thank you, Sue. You're my rock. I don't know what I'd do without you.'

'Right, let's go. Do you know where the bathroom is?'

Sally shook her head and said, 'No.'

'It's up the stairs, second door on the right. And don't be too long. It's not a good idea to stand out.'

42

Sally hurried up an old wooden staircase covered in a multicoloured carpet, restrained by polished brass stair rods that seemed strangely out of place in the modern world. She felt a sudden surge of relief as she reached the landing, its very ordinary appearance giving the moment an unexpected air of normality. But the feeling didn't last. She threw up on entering the bathroom and continued vomiting until there was nothing left but green, acidic bile.

Sally washed her mouth out at the sink, looking at herself in the oval wall mirror, mourning the situation in which she found herself. She briefly considered clambering through the bathroom window and dropping to the ground below. But she dismissed the idea almost immediately. The window was too small and the drop too far.

Sally used the toilet, flushed, washed her hands, and then sat back on the seat, asking herself what to do for the best as the seconds ticked by. She eventually came to a decision. Not an easy decision, not a decision that made everything better, but a decision nonetheless. And that, Sally decided, was progress.

Sally stood on quivery legs, still asking herself if she was doing the right thing. It was a gamble, she knew that. A throw of the dice that had the potential to go horribly wrong. But it was a risk she was prepared to take. She took her smartphone from a trouser pocket and looked at it for a few agonising seconds before finally deciding to act.

Oh shit, no signal.

She moved nearer the window, and then there it was, one bar. A weak signal, but still a signal. She dialled 999 with a fast-moving finger, requesting the police in rushed, hushed, breathy tones as she fought the impulse to throw up again. She was feeling a gut-wrenching combination of relief and apprehension when put through to the West Wales Constabulary control room within seconds of making her call.

'I need to speak to Inspector Kesey, please, it's urgent. It– it couldn't be more urgent. It's life and death.'

Sally listened to the response as her apprehension rose to a new and fearful high. 'No– no, it has to be Laura Kesey. I know her. It's Lewis, Sergeant Lewis. You've got to help me. He's– he's going to be murdered. For fuck's sake, put me through!'

Come on, come on, come on, answer the fucking thing... Oh, thank God!

Sally heard Kesey's familiar Brummie voice at the other end of the line. She explained the situation and location in a faltering voice. She could hear the urgency in Kesey's tone as the detective asked her rushed questions, which Sally answered without hesitation, keeping her voice low for fear of being over-heard. 'No– no, I can't leave my phone on. I can't get out of the house either. I've got to go back downstairs. I'm scared, Laura. Ivy'll be wondering where I am. She controls everything.'

There was a knock on the bathroom door just as Kesey said there was help on the way. Sally dropped the phone to the floor, picked it up, and then switched it off before returning it to her pocket. She was praying no-one had been listening as she slowly opened the bathroom door a few inches at a time. She peered out with startled eyes to see Sue standing on the landing with an impatient look on her face.

'What the hell have you been doing?'

Sally wiped away her tears. 'Sorry, I've got the shits.'

Sue sighed. 'It's time to get back down there.'

'Will you stay close?'

Sue took Sally's hand, leading her across the landing towards the staircase. 'We're going to go down there together, and you're going to do everything I do. Do you hear me? You've got to be brave. He's just a man who got in the way.'

'Okay.'

'Remember, you're a tiger. Tigers don't cry. Sharpen your claws. The world should hear you roar.'

43

Kesey rang Ivy's doorbell just the once, waiting less than twenty-seconds before ordering a burly, six-foot-three-inch, sixteen-stone constable to break the door down. PC Rob Hughes swung the steel battering ram, or the big red key as it was more commonly known as in the force, shattering the lock and fracturing the wooden frame in two places. One more powerful blow and the door flew open, allowing Kesey to enter the cottage first, followed by Hughes, and then three other uniformed constables, two men and a woman.

They all heard an ambulance siren getting gradually louder as they crossed the lounge in search of Lewis. Kesey opened the kitchen door first, finding the entrance to the cellar only seconds later.

The cellar light was off now, and the room in total silence. Kesey asked herself if Sally's call had been correct as she looked down into the gloom. She shouted out Lewis' name, 'Ray!' once, then again, louder and more insistent this time, but all was silent. A pervasive silence that seemed to echo around the stone building.

Kesey turned to her subordinates, speaking in urgent tones

intended to convey her concern. 'Rob, with me, the rest of you, I want every inch of this place searched. Start upstairs and work down. If you find anything, call out immediately. If Sergeant Lewis is here, I want him found.'

Kesey located the cellar's light switch within seconds. She could feel her chest tightening as she began slowly descending the concrete steps, with Hughes close behind. When Kesey entered the cellar, she was greeted by the strange sight of six women huddled together in one corner to the side of the entrance, all of whom were staring directly at her. Ivy was standing at the far side of the windowless room immediately next to Lewis's flabby, milk-white body. She had a syringe clutched tightly in her right hand.

Kesey turned to Hughes, ordering him to lead the six women up the steps and into the lounge, where they would be arrested and detained. He followed instructions, calling out for backup as he went. The six women complied without a word of objection, filing up the steps in single order one after another with blank, expressionless faces that gave nothing away.

Kesey focused on Ivy and only Ivy, walking slowly towards her and stopping about six feet from where she stood. The detective looked directly into the older woman's eyes, trying to decide between persuasion or attack. Persuasion won out, at least for the moment. 'I want you to drop the syringe. Don't do anything stupid. You're in enough trouble without making it worse for yourself.'

'I guess it's over then. That's it, my work's done.'

Kesey took another step forward, ever so slowly, ever so carefully. 'Drop the syringe, Ivy. Drop it to the floor and kick it towards me. There'll be plenty of time to talk later.'

'I never wanted to kill Raymond, not really. It was nothing personal. He got in the way, that's all.'

Kesey rocked slightly in one place. She looked down at

Lewis, relieved to see his chest moving ever so slightly. She asked herself if she'd imagined it, seeing what she wanted to see. But, no, the movement was definitely there. 'What have you done to him?'

Ivy threw the syringe aside. 'He's drugged, sedated, no more than that. You arrived just in time. Although, you have no idea of the damage you've done.' She held her hands out in front of her. 'I assume you'll want to arrest me. Take me away. I'm the guilty one, the *only* guilty one.'

Kesey moved quickly now, securing Ivy's wrists in steel handcuffs and shoving her towards the base of the steps. She cautioned her prisoner in line with the rules of evidence, and then called out, 'Get back down here, Rob, and get this bitch out of here. Are the paramedics up there?'

'Yes, ma'am!'

Kesey barked out her order. 'Tell them it's safe to come down.'

Ivy was marched up the steps towards a waiting police car, followed by the paramedics, who struggled to carry Lewis up the steep steps on an overburdened stretcher. Kesey stayed with her sergeant the entire time, ensuring his modesty was covered, watching with teary eyes as the paramedics did their job with speed and efficiency.

She'd never felt more helpless; never more ill at ease. Kesey was regretting not having listened to her sergeant's suspicions more than she'd ever regretted anything before.

Please be all right, Ray. Please be all right.

44

Kesey sat alongside a younger subordinate, with Ivy and her experienced lawyer sitting on the opposite side of the interview room table. Specialist audio equipment was recording the process.

Kesey stated the time, date and location, speaking slowly and clearly, and then continued, her tone conveying the seriousness with which she was treating the interview. The legal rules mattered. There was no room for error. She had to get everything right. 'My name is Detective Inspector Laura Kesey. Also present is Detective Constable Tanya Evans, the suspect Ms Ivy Breen, and her solicitor, Mr Trevor Anderson. I need to remind you, Ms Breen, that you are still subject to caution. Anything you say could be used in evidence in any future court proceedings. Do you understand?'

Ivy looked past Kesey, then the recording equipment, and then at the wall again. She appeared agitated, making abrupt, fitful movements with her hands, but there was a determination about her too. A stoic quality that concerned Kesey more than she thought it should. Ivy spoke directly to the microphone rather than to the detectives. As if they didn't matter. As if they weren't in the room at all.

Ivy coughed twice before speaking. 'I would like to make it clear that I have no intention whatsoever of answering any questions, whatever their source. I will simply say "no comment" to anything asked of me. I would, however, like to share a prepared statement which presents the full and relevant facts. I will read it out loud for the benefit of the recording. I need to be sure that my actual words are a matter of record. I have good reason not to trust the police.'

Kesey's frustration and irritation were revealed by her tone as she addressed the solicitor, 'I need your client to confirm she understands the legal position. This is a murder investigation. It doesn't get any more serious than that.'

He made a written note before replying. 'My client has made her position perfectly clear. Can we get on with it please?'

Kesey decided there was nothing to gain by objecting. It was a battle she couldn't win. 'When you're ready, Ms Breen.'

Ivy closed her eyes for a beat and then opened them before speaking. She still didn't look directly at either officer, but instead stared either at her lawyer, the recording equipment, or one wall or another. 'I wish to make a full and frank confession. I killed Aled Harper. I took Beth's car without her consent or knowledge, and I ran him over as he jogged along a dark country road near to the seaside village of Ferryside.

'I also killed Timothy Garvey in a Cardiff hotel. I stabbed him multiple times until he was dead.

'No-one else took part, and no-one other than my victims was aware of my actions until now. I acted alone at every stage. If you dig up my back garden, you will find two more adult male bodies, the identities of which I will leave it to you to discover. I killed both unidentified men, I dismembered the bodies in the cellar of my home, and I buried the body parts under the rose bushes bordering the lawn. All my actions were the result of the failure of the authorities to adequately deal with crimes of violence against women and children. I feel no regret and I would do the same again in the same circumstances.'

Ivy paused to catch her breath. 'Finally, I also confirm that I drugged Sergeant Raymond Lewis before imprisoning him in my cellar. None of the other women found at my home were aware of my actions until their arrival earlier this evening. I fully intended to kill Raymond to avoid detection, but the other women prevented me from doing so. Everything I've told you is a true record of events. I have made this confession of my own free will. That is the end of my sworn statement. I have nothing further to add, other than that I'll be pleading guilty when these matters come to court.'

Kesey didn't believe a word of it. But she knew there was little she could do. When she asked further questions or requested further detail or clarification, Ivy simply said, 'No comment' as she'd said she would. Kesey persevered for almost an hour before finally throwing in the towel.

'Switch the recording off, Tanya. Let's get her charged. This interview is at an end.'

45

Kesey approached Lewis' hospital bed with a bag of seedless grapes in one hand and a local daily newspaper in the other. She smiled broadly on seeing that her sergeant was sitting up and chatting to a plump, red-faced staff nurse in a light-blue uniform, who seemed to find everything he said surprisingly amusing. Kesey acknowledged the nurse with a nod of her head and then pulled up a seat, as the nurse walked away to attend to another patient.

'It's good to see you again, Ray. I thought I might never see you again the last time I was here. It was touch-and-go for a while. You were in one hell of a state.'

'I had a bad reaction to the drug. I'm stuck here for another week at least.'

'You behave yourself and do what you're told. Just be glad they're looking after you. Don't even *think* about discharging yourself early. I know what you're like.'

He stuffed three grapes into his mouth. 'Have you found out where Ivy got the sedative?'

'We're still looking into it.'

'Who've you charged?'

Kesey shuffled her feet. 'Investigations are ongoing. I think that's the best way of putting it.'

'Who, Laura, who? What aren't you telling me?'

'We've only charged Ivy. The CPS isn't interested in anyone else.'

His eyes widened. 'What? How the fuck did that happen?'

'Ivy confessed to everything, Pearson's death apart, for obvious reasons. And all the other women said, "No comment" to every single question asked, even Sally, who saved your life. She told me what she felt she had to on the phone and that was it.'

'There is no way all that happened by coincidence.'

'They agreed on a strategy in advance. They had time. It's the only thing that makes any sense. Say nothing and leave the talking to Ivy. She sacrificed herself for the group. It's as simple as that. I know her claims are bullshit, the others were definitely involved, but try proving it.'

'She'll go down for a very long time.'

'There were two more bodies in the garden. That's a full life sentence.'

He frowned hard. 'Who were they?'

'Harry Smith, Beth's ex, was one, the other's a work in progress. He'd been down there quite some time. The place was like a boneyard. Both bodies were cut to pieces, saw marks on the bones, the lot.'

Lewis shook his head, grimacing. 'I thought Ivy was one of the good guys.'

'She had everyone conned.'

'Fancy a grape?'

Kesey shook her head. 'How are the stitches? I bet they're stinging a bit. Your head still looks pretty swollen.'

He touched his scalp and grinned. 'I'm just relieved the fracture didn't ruin my good looks.'

Kesey wiped away a tear. 'I'm so glad you're safe, Ray. It nearly broke my heart when I saw you lying there in that cellar.'

'Did I mention that I was right all along?'

She rolled her eyes. 'Oh, here we go. You were *partly* right, that's the truth of it. You didn't work everything out.'

'You should have listened to me.'

'Gut feelings aren't evidence. You know that as well as I do.'

'Yeah, but I *was* right.'

'Yes, Ray, you *were* right. Are you happy now? Is that what you wanted to hear?'

He grinned mischievously. 'I may remind you of that once or twice when I'm back in work.'

'I'll look forward to that. I suspect you'll be banging on about it until you finally retire.'

Lewis laughed. 'How's the family?'

'I've promised Jan a holiday somewhere warm when the court case is over. Tenerife maybe, or Lanzarote: you can fly from Cardiff.'

'How's Halliday? Have the two of you kissed and made up?'

'There was a rumour he was going back to London. But it turned out to be wishful thinking.'

'Shame.'

Kesey stood, pushing her chair back. 'Right, I'd better make a move. You need your rest.'

'I'm going to thank Sally personally when I get the chance. I may even buy her some chocolates. A nice big box and a card.'

'You do that, Ray, but maybe leave Sue alone. That wouldn't be a bad idea in the circumstances.'

'Really?'

'Yes, *really*, and that's an order.'

Lewis raised a hand to the side of his head in mock salute as he had many times before. 'Yes, ma'am, anything you say, ma'am.'

'I could swing for you sometimes.'

'No, seriously, thanks for coming, Laura, it's appreciated.'

Kesey waved before walking away. 'I'll be in again tomorrow. Someone's got to keep an eye on you. Now get some sleep.'

EPILOGUE

Susan Johnson sat on a two-seater red leather sofa in her small, dank Bristol bedsit about six months later, a bottle of Irish whiskey in one hand and some pill packets on the coffee table in front of her. She looked from one to the other as her dark mood beat her down a little further, one depressive thought after another bombarding her troubled mind in an unstoppable flood she'd feared impossible to stop. She felt no guilt for her crimes, and certainly no remorse. She still believed she'd done nothing but good, a worthy thing, a service to her kind. But happiness seemed beyond her. She loathed the person she'd become. Ivy's imprisonment had been a blow she still wasn't over, and leaving the refuge the last straw. She'd now been living alone with her demons for almost four months. And that, she'd decided, was more than she could handle. Sue needed a friend. Someone who'd been there. Someone who understood. She looked across at Karen Hoyle with a look of utter dejection, sad, but glad to see a familiar face.

'Thanks so much for coming, Karen. I really appreciate your support. I know we all agreed to avoid contact, to get on with our lives as best we could, but I was desperate. I didn't know where else to turn.'

The social worker forced a thin smile. 'It's not a problem. It's only a couple of hours drive down the motorway. I'm just glad you picked up the phone when you did.'

'I don't think I'd be here now if I hadn't.'

'I'm delighted we've had the chance to talk. The last hour's flown by. I've missed you.'

'Yes, yes it has. I've missed you too.'

Karen reached out, gripping Sue's hand, holding it tight. 'There's better times ahead, my friend. Suicide's not the answer. We'll get through this together. I'll even transfer to Bristol if I need to. Whatever it takes.'

Sue took a swig of whiskey. 'Sally sent me a letter. The compensation came through. She's living on a commune in Devon a few miles from the sea. My little one loves it. It's off-grid, there's lots of other children, exactly what he needs.'

Karen handed Sue a paper hankie to wipe away her tears. 'Are you still *certain* you did the right thing? Giving up a child is a huge decision, even if the authorities are ignorant of the facts. I'm sure Sally would understand if you wanted him back. She may even be expecting it.'

Sue pushed the pills away, the packets falling to the floor. 'No, that's the one thing I am sure about. Sally's brilliant with him. She'll be a better mother than I could ever be. It's good for her and good for my little one too. Everyone's going to think he's her child. She can give him the happy life I couldn't.'

'I've always thought you an excellent mother.'

Sue looked away. 'I've seen too much, done too much. I'm broken; something's missing. There's no point trying to deny it. I need to focus on myself. I need to find a way to repair if life's going to go on...'

'As long as you're certain.'

'The Sisterhood gave life purpose, but that's over now. I have to find a different path. Maybe when he's older he'll want to meet me. I'll be satisfied with that.'

'People can change, you'll change, I think that process has already begun. Our conversation is testament to that.'

Sue took another swig of the strong spirit, grimacing as it burnt her throat. 'I'm alive, I've got a friend to talk to, and no more killing. I guess that's progress. Maybe it will stay that way. For now I'll be happy with that.'

THE END

CPSIA information can be obtained
at www.ICGtesting.com
Printed in the USA
JSHW041454100122
21912JS00002B/252

9 781913 419882